SHATTERED DREAMS

One moment of selflessness had seen Simon Clarke's dreams shattered forever. Slowly, he was rebuilding his life. Heather Marshall had lived through a nightmare experience with her daughter, Amy. The memories of the past still haunt her present. Can Simon and Heather learn to trust and love again? The threat of new tragedy tests their fledgling reawakening. Will the promise of new dreams be shattered or is there hope for a future — together?

Books by Margaret McDonagh
in the Linford Romance Library:

HIDDEN LOVE
(RUTHLESS HEART)
FULL CIRCLE
SWEET REVENGE
BROKEN HEARTS
FORBIDDEN LOVE
JOURNEY INTO LOVE
SHADOWS OF THE PAST
WEB OF DECEIT
A GAME OF LOVE
CUPID'S ARROW

MARGARET McDONAGH

SHATTERED DREAMS

Complete and Unabridged

LINFORD
Leicester

First published in Great Britain in 1998

First Linford Edition
published 2003

British Library CIP Data

McDonagh, Margaret
    Shattered dreams.—Large print ed.—
Linford romance library
1. Love stories
2. Large type books
I. Title
823.9'14 [F]

ISBN 0–7089–4929–0

Published by
F. A. Thorpe (Publishing)
Anstey, Leicestershire

Set by Words & Graphics Ltd.
Anstey, Leicestershire
Printed and bound in Great Britain by
T. J. International Ltd., Padstow, Cornwall

This book is printed on acid-free paper

1

Simon Clarke swung to and fro in his high-backed chair, a brooding pout on his face. Money, he thought — it brought everything, everything but health and happiness. He had plenty of money. Far more than he knew what to do with. And who but he knew better about health and happiness . . . or the lack of it?

He looked around his comfortable office, thought of his plush apartment, his petrol-hungry, custom-built sports car. What was the use of any of it when he was only living half a life? Money, or what it bought, didn't keep him warm at night, didn't ease his loneliness, his pain. And it certainly couldn't bring back the only real reason he had ever had for living.

Pain burned unceasingly in his right shoulder. He raised a hand, absently, uselessly, kneading against the ache, the stiffness. He waited for it to ease, lost in his dark thoughts.

He had never appreciated the proverbial silver spoon in the mouth he had been born with, nor the title, nor the double-barrelled name. He was his own man, he acknowledged. He didn't need to hide behind family tradition to make something of his life — not the life he'd had before, not the life he had now.

Thinking of the barbed words, the snide comments about his chosen path, the so-called friends with feet of clay, brought a soft curse to his lips.

'I'd go crazy doing nothing,' he confided to the empty room.

Fate had robbed him of the life he had craved, had shattered all his dreams, but that didn't mean he had to sit back, pander to family tradition, stagnate. Children's voices broke through his dark reverie. He swung his chair round from his desk and looked out of the windows of his office over the school grounds. Lunch time already? A frown furrowed his forehead.

The kids were OK, he thought, the beginnings of a smile lightening his sombre expression. As he watched them stream out of the building, laughing, playing, gathering in groups, he wondered again why they were drawn to him, why he seemed to have this affinity with children.

It had been reluctant at first, on his part at least. When he had been trying to put his life back together, he could have made a grand gesture, have gone to some inner city trouble spot, made a statement, changed the world. A self-derisive laugh escaped. He'd run out of grand gestures.

Instead, he had chosen to come here, to the rambling, old school on the hill, filled with children from three to thirteen, day pupils and boarders, children who came from wealthy families. He knew these kids because he had been one of them. He knew their backgrounds, understood the many who came happily because it was better than home. They had everything money could buy. But not all of them had love, companionship, someone who listened and did not trample on their dreams. He listened.

When the school had been in financial trouble and threatened with closure, he had stepped in. He had found people to run it, to staff it, to back it. He had invested his own time, his money, what remained of his life, to give something to the children everyone imagined wanted for nothing. But he knew better. He understood hearts that yearned for affection, for understanding, for a place to be important. He knew, because he had once been one of them.

If he could help the kids make the best out of themselves, if he could encourage and cherish and nurture the hopes of the young, then at least he was doing something worthwhile, giving something back. Before, he had only taken, as if it was his due.

As his watchful gaze scanned the

playground a motionless, lonely figure captured his attention. He had noticed the child before. She was always alone, always aloof, always . . . unhappy? Perhaps not unhappy, he decided with a deepening frown, perhaps just unapproachable. Was it the child who drew him or his empathy with the emotions she displayed? He rose stiffly to his feet and moved nearer to the window.

She couldn't be more than five. He didn't know her name. The tots didn't come within his educational orbit, but he did know she had only arrived at the school that term. She was the most exquisitely beautiful child he had ever seen, Simon admitted. Something about her tugged at his heartstrings, awakened in him some kind of protective instinct, her separateness affecting him because he recognised it only too well.

With an impatient sigh, he left his office and walked out of the building into the late October sunshine. As always, the nagging pain accompanied him wherever he went, a constant reminder, a constant torment. He had scarcely been outside for a minute before he was surrounded by children. Smiling, he listened to their incessant chatter, his gaze wandering over their heads, locking on to his little pixie.

She was sitting on a low wall studying the burnished oak leaf she held in her small fingers with aching concentration. Her dark hair seemed to shine like polished ebony in the autumn sunlight, her elfin face hauntingly solemn.

'Mr Clarke?'

A hand tugged insistently at the sleeve of his tracksuit top.

'Mr Clarke, will you come and see my new bike?'

He glanced down into the eager, freckled face of the ten-year-old boy who still clung to his arm.

'Sure, Johnny.'

Allowing himself to be ushered towards the sheds, surrounded by his youthful entourage, he flicked a final look back at the girl on the wall. His footsteps slowed. Resisting the children's calls to hurry, he watched as several other girls jostled the lonely child. He could not hear what they were saying, but she looked frightened. Extracting his arm from Johnny's hold, he turned back.

'I'll be with you later, OK?' he murmured over his shoulder as he set off to rescue his little pixie.

Before he had gone half a dozen strides, one of the other girls appeared to push her. She lost her balance, and with a small scream, tumbled backwards over the wall and on to the concrete surrounding the netball courts. Seeing his approach, the other girls ran off. Anger coiling inside him, noticing who the culprits were for attention later, he hurried down the grassy bank and kneeled down beside the child who still lay on the ground. He could see a trickle of blood seeping out of her hair and beginning to trail a line down one pale cheek.

She looked up at him through wounded blue eyes that swum with tears. Mistrust was reflected in their stormy depths, and loneliness. Simon felt crushed. With infinite gentleness, he smiled, then lifted her up in his arms, ignoring the scream of protest from his shoulder.

Her small body felt stiff in his arms. She didn't immediately wind her arms around his neck as one of the other children would have done, he noticed, sad that a child so young should be so aloof. Uncaring about the blood that was now staining his top, he held her protectively on the journey across the school yard, inside the building and along to the first aid room. Tentatively, her arms crept around him, uncertainty in those eyes that looked to him like winter pansies washed with rain.

'Hush, poppet,' he soothed, as a few sobs shuddered through her.

He eased her down to sit on the table, then smiled and softly tapped a finger on the tip of her nose.

'You're going to be fine.'

She wiped the back of one hand over her damp cheeks.

'I want Mummy.'

'We'll call Mummy soon,' he reassured her, reaching out to examine the damage to her head.

'It hurts.'

'I'm sure it does, poppet. That was a nasty tumble you took.'

Gently he assessed the damage, discovering a nasty cut on her scalp that would definitely need stitching. He cleaned it and applied a temporary dressing, concerned that the child be properly examined at hospital after such a blow to her head.

'What's your name?' he asked, trying to keep her mind occupied.

'Amy.'

She sucked on one thumb and looked at him with shy, tear-damp eyes.

'What's yours?'

'Simon. Simon Clarke. Do you have a last name?'

She nodded and again spoke past her thumb.

'Marshall,' she whispered.

'Well, Amy Marshall, we'll have ourselves a little adventure, and we'll ask Mummy to join us, OK?'

Wondering where the school nurse was, Simon reached for the telephone and called the office extension. After discovering the nurse was off for the afternoon, he instructed the secretary to contact Amy's class teacher.

'Can you call Mrs Marshall when you've done that, Maureen? Have her meet us at Casualty.'

'You're taking her to hospital?' the secretary queried with concern.

'I'm not taking any chances with a head injury, and the cut needs stitching, I think.'

As he hung up the telephone, Amy's teacher, Joan Jeffries, arrived in the first aid room.

'What happened?' she demanded, glancing at the blood-soaked dressing.

Simon explained the details, noting

with concern that Amy did not interact well with her teacher. Instead, she almost seemed to shrink against him, still that unsettling distrust in her clouded eyes. He wondered what the story was.

'I'm taking her along to the hospital to be checked over,' he continued, deciding there and then that he would be responsible for Amy's well-being and not entrust her care to someone else, someone she appeared less comfortable with.

Feeling the child's hand creep into his, he glanced down at her, something tightening inside him at this small sign of trust.

'Maureen is arranging for Mrs Marshall to meet us there.'

'If she can locate her. Amy's mother is a busy woman,' Joan Jeffries remarked with some acerbity.

Too busy for her own child, Simon wondered with a flash of irrational anger.

Joan Jeffries reached out towards

Amy, but as the child evaded her touch, her expression tightened and her hand fell away.

'Well,' she commented as she walked towards the door, 'I don't envy you. She's a difficult child. I can't seem to get through to her.'

No, Simon thought as the middle-aged woman left the room, I'm not surprised with an attitude like that. Amy would need careful handling, quiet patience and understanding, to be coaxed out of her shell.

Vowing to take more interest in the goings-on of the younger children at the school, in his capacity as a director and governor as well as a physical education teacher, Simon lifted Amy into his arms and walked out to his car.

He settled the child in the seat, ensuring she was securely and safely fastened in, then he crunched round the gravel and slid behind the wheel. The engine gave a quiet roar as it fired to life. Selecting first gear, he eased the car down the hill.

For a while Amy was silent, her presence beside him betrayed only by the occasional sob, or the noisy sucking of her thumb. Simon glanced across at her, disturbed by her remoteness, the aching vulnerability to her. He wondered what kind of home she came from, who her parents were, what had happened in her life to make her so painfully alone.

'How are you feeling, poppet?' he asked as he turned the car on to the main road in the direction of the hospital. 'Is your head still hurting?'

The little dark head bobbed in confirmation.

'Do you feel sick or dizzy?'

'No. Will Mummy come soon?'

Simon tried to ignore the way her chin wobbled.

'I'm sure she will. I'll take care of you until she gets here, OK?'

Her head bobbed again, and then she raised her face, her eyes wide, the faintest sign of a shy smile pulling at her mouth.

'I like you.'

'Why, thank you, Amy. I like you, too.'

He felt honoured. Amy did not strike him as a child who gave her trust and friendship easily. He imagined few people were close to her.

'Have you got any guinea pigs?'

Her sudden enquiry took him by surprise and he banked down a laugh.

'No, no, I don't have any pets. Do you?'

'I have two guinea pigs. I did have three but one died.'

'I'm sorry.'

It was the longest sentence he had ever heard her make. Encouraged, he kept her talking.

'What are their names?'

'Ginger. That's 'cos she's ginger-coloured,' she informed him gravely. 'And there's Patch, 'cos she's white and has a black patch over one eye.'

'Do you have other animals?'

Amy shook her head and sucked her thumb for a brief moment.

'I want a puppy but Mummy says it's not prac — '

She frowned in puzzled annoyance and looked at him.

'Practical?' Simon supplied for her, swallowing another smile.

The child nodded vigorously.

'She says he would be lonely at home on his own all day.'

'That makes sense. You wouldn't want him to be lonely, would you?'

'No. But I would love him. Animals are my friends.'

A painful lump lodged itself in Simon's throat. Her simple words, the longing in her voice, reflected all too clearly her own solitude, her craving for love and companionship. More deeply affected than he wanted to be, he was relieved when the hospital came into view. Somehow, he didn't think it was going to be easy to simply get Amy patched up, taken home, and then put her out of his mind.

2

'Mrs Marshall, thank goodness you're back! I tried to reach you at the factory, but you'd already left.'

The rise of panic in the young assistant's voice brought Heather up short. She halted in the centre of the boutique, the in-built fear that refused to ever vanish completely now tightening her nerves to knots.

'What's happened, Jane?' she questioned, controlling the quaver of alarm in her voice with difficulty.

She was over-reacting, she attempted to convince herself as she waited for her junior assistant to elaborate.

'The school phoned, I — '

'Amy? Is it Amy? Is she sick?' Heather interrupted.

'She took a tumble, cut herself. The secretary said one of the teachers had taken her to hospital for a check up.'

'Oh, no!'

Heather hurried through to her office at the rear of her exclusive lingerie boutique and dropped her bag and the samples she was carrying on to her desk.

'How long ago did they phone, Jane?'

'About an hour and a half ago, maybe two. I didn't know how long you'd be. I'm sure she'll be fine, Ms Marshall. The secretary said it was just a standard precaution.'

Worried about her daughter, unwilling to be pacified, Heather bit her lip. Until she held Amy in her arms, until she could see for herself that her precious daughter was unharmed, she could not help but worry. Reaching for the telephone, she called the school.

'I haven't heard from Mr Clarke since he took Amy to the hospital, Ms Marshall,' the secretary informed her.

Amy was alone with some man she didn't know? Taking several deep breaths, Heather damped down her raging anxiety.

'Mr Clarke?'

'He's a director and governor of the school, Ms Marshall, and a part-time teacher here.'

Heather had never met him, and her concern made her doubly wary.

'Why didn't the nurse or Amy's form teacher take her?' she demanded, aware her voice was tight but unable to soften her tone.

'Mr Clarke was there when the accident happened. He tended to Amy.'

'Which hospital did they go to?'

When she had the information, she found the telephone number and rang the casualty department only to learn that Amy had been attended to and was now on her way back to the school. At least the news on her injury was encouraging — a cut that had needed stitching, but no other apparent damage. Replacing the receiver, she snatched up her bag.

'Jane, I'm sorry to do this to you, but you'll have to manage here on your own until Sally comes back from the dentist,' she said in a harassed tone.

'I'll be fine, Ms Marshall. It's been quiet today,' the girl assured her.

Heather nodded. Although young and inclined to fuss in a crisis, Jane was a good assistant. With Amy hurt, she had no option but to leave the shop in the assistant's care.

'Thanks, Jane. I'll call you, and I'll be back as soon as I can.'

'OK, Ms Marshall. I hope Amy is all right.'

Hurrying out to her car, Heather offered up silent prayers. Amy had to be all right, and there was no point in her getting flustered over what appeared on the surface to be a normal, youthful accident. No reason at all to imagine that anything more sinister could be behind it.

Waiting at the traffic lights to turn on to the main road, Heather closed her eyes briefly. She had to stop looking over her shoulder, imagining that the past would catch up with them. It was over, finished. So why did she never really feel safe?

* * *

Amy had been so brave at the hospital. Simon smiled down at her, remembering the tremble of her chin when the local anaesthetic had been administered, the flash of moisture in her eyes that she had blinked away.

While the stitching had been completed with the minimum of fuss, he had held her hand, keeping her attention focused on him and not on the doctor's work. He was relieved there was no damage found on the X-ray, no sign of concussion. All being well, Amy would be fine in a few days.

He wondered with increasing annoyance where the mother was. Amy had asked for her several times, but Mrs Marshall had not shown up at the hospital. It was over two hours since he had asked the secretary to call her.

Didn't the woman care about this child?

Simon watched Amy now as she played on the floor of his office, colouring him a picture with some felt-tip pens he had purloined from the stationery cupboard. She had opened up to him in their time together, at least as much as he imagined Amy opened up to anyone. He had no idea of her background, of the causes of her remoteness, but he'd had her talking about her pets, the books she enjoyed, had even made her laugh once or twice. The melodious tinkle had warmed him.

The sound of the telephone ringing on his desk had him straightening and reaching for the receiver.

'Simon Clarke.'

'I missed you when you came back,' the secretary apologised. 'I thought you'd like to know that Heather Marshall called. She's on her way.'

'Thanks, Maureen. Send her straight in.'

He replaced the receiver and kneeled

down beside Amy.

'Good news,' he said gently. 'Your mummy will be here soon.'

'Oh, thank you!' The answering smile was angelic. 'Do you like my drawing?'

'It's lovely,' he praised, admiring the out-of-scale portraits of what he judged to be her two guinea pigs.

She wrote the names underneath each animal with painstaking care.

'Here, it's for you,' she told him earnestly, holding out the paper.

'Why, thank you, Amy!'

He helped her pack away the paper and pens, then he lifted her up to sit on the side of his desk. Her thin legs swung back and forth as she tucked in to the pocket-sized box of raisins she had selected from the hospital shop, chattering away to him between mouthfuls.

Meanwhile, to Heather, the eight-mile drive to the school seemed to take an eternity. When she finally turned in at the gates, she accelerated up the hill towards the large, rambling Georgian building that had housed the private school since its foundation almost one hundred years ago.

The gravel crunched under the tyres as she pulled to a halt by the door that led to the administration offices. Gathering up her bag, she slid from behind the wheel and hurried to the entrance. After a short wait, during which she had announced her identity over the entryphone, the secretary arrived to admit her. As much as she was impatient to see Amy, Heather was grateful for the school's security. It was one of the reasons she had decided to send her daughter here.

'Ms Marshall, hello.'

'Amy? How is she?'

The secretary smiled as she closed the door and ushered her down the corridor, her heels clacking on the polished wood floor.

'They're back, and she's fine. A few stitches. Mr Clarke will tell you all about it, I'm sure. Follow the corridor down and his door is the end one on the left. He is expecting you.'

'Thank you.'

Leaving the other woman, Heather hurried on down the passage, a mix of relief and anxiety warring within her. She just hoped that Amy was not too stressed, not only from her tumble and trip to the hospital, but after being in the company of a stranger. The child was diffident, reserved, aloof.

Heather supposed that was her fault, although she tried not to blame herself for the past. She could cope with anything, even the past, the fear, if only she could keep Amy safe, give her the happiness, the innocence, the freedom that any child deserved.

As she approached the door to Mr Clarke's office, she heard a sudden peal of child's laughter. Amy's laughter! Heather halted in mid-stride, stunned at the sound. True, her daughter was bubbly and talkative at home, her hidden personality emerging, happy and mischievous, when it was just the two of them. But for her to be as relaxed as that, to be comfortable with someone she did not know was astounding.

Walking the last few steps to the door, she tapped and entered, unprepared for the sight of her daughter sitting on the side of a large, cluttered desk, a packet of raisins in one hand and a stack of felt-tip pens in the other. Her eyes were bright with laughter, her mouth pulled in a genuine, happy smile that quite deflected Heather's attention from the dressing along her hairline.

Tears pricked her own eyes, relief that Amy was not seriously injured, and the joy of seeing her so at ease, so normal. She had time to think how awful it was, what it said about their lives, that she should be so moved to see her child smile, hear her laugh, as if it was a thing so rare and wonderful.

Then the man she had scarcely noticed was helping the wriggling child down from the desk, and Amy flew across to her, wrapping her strong, slender arms around her neck. Heather dropped to one knee, holding her daughter close. She stroked the long, soft strands of her hair, kissed her warm cheeks, then pulled back to study the graze on her forehead, then the place where the dressing was fixed.

'I'm sorry I couldn't get here faster, darling,' she murmured, lifting Amy in her arms and settling her against her hip. 'I was stuck in a traffic jam.'

Amy raised one hand to her head, eyes wide.

'I had four stitches,' she announced. 'Simon said I was very brave.'

'I'm sure you were.'

For the first time, Heather directed her attention to the man, assailed by a welter of impressions and emotions. She picked up at once on the flicker of hostility that charged the air between them, the flash of confusion that clouded his eyes. He watched her in silence and she felt she was being judged. She met his forthright gaze, returning his inspection. Several inches above average height, it was a long time since she had been forced to look up at a man. Now she did.

He was tall and broad, with dark hair, those cool, enigmatic eyes, and a strong face, attractive and appealing, the interesting side of handsome. For no good reason she could explain, he intimidated her.

'Mr Clarke?' she assumed, her voice cool.

He inclined his head in brief acknowledgement.

'Nice of you to join us, Mrs Marshall.'

Her awareness sharpened at the barely-veiled sarcasm in his tone, Heather stared at him, failing to correct her title. She opened her mouth to make a sharp retort, then decided she owed him no explanation or excuses.

'Thank you for taking care of Amy,' she said instead. 'Perhaps you could tell me what happened.'

She listened to his clipped version of events, his assurances that action would be taken against the girls who had challenged Amy and caused her to fall, and his account of what had taken place at the hospital.

'The doctor is not anticipating any after effects,' he informed her with a slight softening of his attitude. 'I have his name and contact number for you, and he suggests you make an appointment with your own practitioner. Naturally, if you are worried, or Amy experiences any headaches, dizziness or sickness, you should take her back.'

'Thank you.'

They watched each other for a moment, the tension still humming and making Heather feel awkward.

'Well,' she announced, breaking the uncomfortable silence, and shifting Amy's position, 'I suppose we had better be getting home, young lady.'

Amy wriggled in her hold, struggling to get down. Heather complied, a mix of puzzlement and surprise on her face as she watched her daughter skip across to Simon Clark, tug on his top, and encourage him down for a hug. She noticed the man's ill-disguised wince as Amy bumped his right shoulder. To her amazement, the child gave him a hug, kissing his cheek.

'Thank you for being my friend, and for my raisins and pens,' she whispered softly.

'I was glad to be here, Amy. And thank you for my lovely drawing.'

When Amy returned to her side, Heather reached instinctively for her hand, clasping it to her. She had never seen her daughter so demonstrative, so comfortable with anyone other than herself or her grandparents.

'Goodbye, Mr Clarke, I'm grateful for your help.'

'My pleasure.'

With a brusque nod, Heather led Amy away, conscious of his gaze on her, wondering just what it was about him that set her on edge and made her tense. It was ridiculous to feel threatened, she chastised herself as they left the building and crossed the gravel drive to the car. She strapped Amy into her seat, asking herself if there would ever come a day when she was not constantly looking for ulterior motives, a day when her past no longer coloured her present.

Simon watched from a window across the passage as Amy and her mother drove away. He still felt stunned, uncertain what had gripped him more about Heather Marshall — her stunning beauty, or the unmistakable mistrust and underlying fear in her eyes. Was it fear for her daughter, or something more? Disturbed, he walked back to his office and sat behind his desk, his hand unconsciously straying to the ache in his shoulder. Today had brought back painful reminders. How he hated hospitals. If it hadn't been for Amy, nothing could have dragged him in there.

He had been wrong to question her mother's love, Simon acknowledged. It had been easy to see their bond, the deep caring, the specialness of their relationship. But now he had more questions than ever. Questions that were none of his business. Questions about the fear and remoteness, the wariness, that both mother and daughter shared. What were they scared of?

An annoyed frown puckered his brow. He didn't want to know. He didn't want to ask questions. Most of all, he didn't want to care. But in a short time, Amy had affected him, touched an inner part of him, and as for her mother . . . Simon bit off an angry curse. He couldn't get her out of his mind.

It wasn't just that she was stunning to look at, he told himself, unable to check his wandering thoughts. He had met plenty of beautiful women and none had had this immediate effect on him. It was something else, something indefinable, like an inner recognition. Or perhaps it was just like with Amy, something in him picked up on the aloofness, the aloneness.

Heather Marshall was tall, willowy, the fall of soft dark hair that shadowed one side of her face a shade darker than Amy's. She had looked chic, polished. A gloss had highlighted the tempting curve of her mouth, a hint of mascara lengthening lashes that framed the most incredible eyes he had ever seen. He had a feeling she was somehow familiar, but he was certain he would never have forgotten meeting her before. Simon drew his thoughts up short. She was a married woman, he rebuked himself. What on earth was he doing? With an impatient sigh, he checked his watch, then rose to his feet to head across to the gym.

★　★　★

'And Simon says he never had guinea pigs, but I think he'd like to see mine. Can he, Mummy?'

Heather murmured a noncommittal response and struggled to curb her impatience. If Amy chattered on any more about Simon Clarke, she felt sure she would explode. The man had been kind, she allowed. She was grateful he had looked after Amy, had been able to encourage a response from her reticent child, and she had thanked him. What she did not need was for Amy to develop some kind of misplaced hero worship.

Quite why he had rubbed her the wrong way, Heather was at a loss to explain. Perhaps it was the thread of disapproval, the air of hostility, that had marked her entrance into his office. Perhaps it was the easy way he'd had with her daughter, getting through to her as so few people could. She recalled how his eyes had looked at her, inside her, as if probing her thoughts, assessing her, finding her lacking in some way as a mother. It had rankled, made her angry.

Approaching the house she and Amy had shared for the last eighteen months, Heather turned into the drive and activated the device that opened the electronically controlled gates between the high brick walls that ringed the property. She drove the car straight into the garage, the doors gliding home behind them. Stepping out, she unstrapped Amy's seat belt and held the door open as her child slid out, still clutching her pens and the now empty box of raisins. Taking her bag and Amy's school box from the back seat, she opened the door to the kitchen and ushered Amy inside.

'Mummy, can I have an apple?'

Heather set her things on the kitchen worktop. Handing her daughter the fruit, Heather smiled back, hugging her close for a moment.

'I don't want you rushing about outside until we see how you're feeling, understand?'

'OK.'

She crunched into her apple and reached for the door handle.

'Can I just go and see Ginger and Patch?'

'All right, sweetheart, but remember what I said.'

'Yes, Mummy.'

Heather watched from the kitchen window as Amy hurried outside, then remembering the instructions, she slowed to a more sedate pace and glanced guiltily over her shoulder. Seeing she was being watched, she grinned again and waved. Heather smothered a laugh. She was such a precious child. When she had crossed the secluded, secure garden to the run that housed the guinea pigs and their palatial hutch, Heather sat down at the table and took out the hospital number Simon Clarke had given her.

After checking thoroughly the information on Amy's injury and acquainting herself with the signs to look out for, she next rang her general practitioner to make an appointment for Amy to have her stitches removed in a week's time. She then made herself a cup of strong tea and then checked in with the boutique. Sally, her manageress, was back in charge and all appeared fine. Heather felt content not to go back in until Amy was better and had returned to school.

Thinking of the school concentrated her mind once more on Simon Clarke. Now that she thought about it, his name rang a vague bell, although she had never met him when she had looked over the school before enrolling Amy. She remembered that he was co-owner, a director of the business, and, as the secretary had reminded her, he was also a governor and involved on the teaching side in some capacity. There should be no reason whatever for her to feel nervous of him or his apparent rapport with Amy. Even so, she found it difficult to banish the inner disquiet that had become such a feature of her life.

Checking on Amy again and seeing her sitting in the run playing with her furry friends, Heather opened her address book and thumbed to a number she hadn't called for some months. With a frown, she reached for the telephone again. The call was answered after several rings, the voice brusque, impatient, the Irish accent heavy and familiar.

'Murphy, it's Heather Marshall.'

'Heather, how are you?' the man asked, his tone softening. 'Nothing's wrong, is it?'

She was quick to reassure him.

'No, we're doing fine, Murphy, on the whole.'

She went on to tell him about Amy's new school, and about the events that day.

'I know I'm being unreasonable, but I'd just feel happier if I knew something more about him.'

'Consider it done. I'll get back to you.'

'Thanks, Murphy.'

Heather was unsure if she felt relieved or foolish when she replaced the receiver. Murphy O'Sullivan had been watching out for them for the last two years, and she was conscious that she could all too easily come to use him as an emotional crutch. She had so nearly been guilty of that in the early days, those dark days when the fear had dogged her every step.

Now she had to believe she was free of that, had to get on with life, for her own sake as well as Amy's. But it was easier said than done. Her self-confidence, her sense of her own worth and belief in her judgement of people and situations had taken a tremendous battering. Perhaps it was still too soon for her to step out into the big wide world unaided. With Amy to consider, it was not worth taking any risks.

Simon was not surprised when he discovered that Amy Marshall was absent from school the next day. What did surprise him was just how much time thoughts of her, and her mother, seemed to occupy his mind, despite his determination to push the whole incident aside. It was a long time since he had allowed himself to think about a woman — Eileen.

A dark frown creased his forehead, the old, familiar and bitter disenchantment tightening a knot inside him. The memories, bad memories, should have been consigned to the past, forgotten, no longer allowed to hurt. But the hurt, the anger were still there, festering. And so was the determination he would never be caught out again. Drumming his fingers on the desk top, Simon's mood darkened. No-one would play with his emotions again. He had been naïve, he admitted. But all that was in the past. He didn't need anyone, least of all a woman, to make his life more complete.

So why couldn't he get Heather Marshall out of his mind? He didn't need this. She was stand-offish, aloof, married with a young daughter. He had no business thinking about her, about the way she had looked. Frustrated, he ran his fingers through his hair. A tap on his door diverted his attention.

'Come in.'

'We missed you in the staff room' the secretary said, smiling as she entered the office. 'I've brought you a cup of coffee.'

'Thanks, Maureen. I thought I'd try to get through some of this paper work before my first class.'

He sipped the strong, sweet coffee she had brought him.

'Maureen,' he called, halting her as she walked to the door. 'The Marshall girl,' he began.

The secretary came back and sat in a chair opposite him.

'What about her? She's all right, isn't she?'

'As far as I know, she'll be fine. I just wondered what you knew about her. She seemed withdrawn. I noticed she didn't communicate well with her form mistress.'

'I don't know very much. I've heard some talk.'

'What kind of talk?' he demanded, his curiosity roused.

'Joan Jeffries is a wonderful teacher of the little ones, but she likes things to run smoothly, everything to follow a pattern,' Maureen said.

'Go on,' Simon encouraged as

Maureen paused, clearly concerned she was gossiping. 'This goes no further than my office.'

'Well, Amy Marshall is different. She doesn't fit into standard patterns, and I think Joan finds that difficult to deal with.'

'So what you are saying is that a child with special needs, emotional needs, one like Amy, who is reserved, apart from the other children, tends not to be so easily accepted by Joan.'

'Sort of. Yes, I suppose so.' Maureen paused again. 'She loves all the children, but I think she finds it harder to interact with those like Amy.'

'Do you know anything of the child's background?'

'Not really, no. From what I've seen and heard, Amy is distant, and it is hard to get past that outer shell. She has no real friends in her class. Her mother is much the same. She's polite, caring, but she keeps herself to herself. When I spoke with her yesterday, she was very concerned. That was understandable, but she seemed overly anxious when I said you had taken her to the hospital.'

'Really? In what way?' Simon questioned with a frown.

'She asked why the nurse, or Joan Jeffries, hadn't taken her. She seemed panicky, not knowing who you were.'

Would that explain the edge of fear he had detected, Simon wondered.

'She's such an attractive woman, isn't she?' Maureen continued conversationally. 'She runs a boutique, 'Next to Nothing.' She used to be in fashion, probably a model.'

'What about the father?'

Maureen frowned.

'I've never seen him, or spoken to him. I don't think Amy ever talks about her family. Are you concerned?'

Simon didn't know what he was, only that he was asking questions he had no business to, thinking things about Heather Marshall that were detrimental to his peace of mind.

'No,' he replied now, forcing a smile. 'I was just curious. Amy seemed aloof, lonely. I wondered what the story was, that's all.'

With a relieved smile, Maureen rose to her feet.

'I'll leave you now, then. Back to the paper work!'

'Right.' Simon laughed. 'Thanks again for the coffee. I appreciate it.'

When the secretary had gone, he returned his attention to the reports on his desk, but his concentration continued to waver. Absently, he rubbed at the perpetual ache in his shoulder and upper arm.

Whatever answers he found to his questions about Amy and her mother only seemed to produce more questions. Despite all his determination to put them from his mind, he could not shake the disturbing belief that something was not quite right in the Marshalls' world.

3

'I'm sending the information you wanted through by fax,' Murphy O'Sullivan's brogue relayed to Heather's answerphone. 'Let me know if there's anything else you're wanting, Heather. Keep in touch, now. And give that wee scoundrel my best.'

Smiling, Heather switched off the machine. She had taken Amy with her to the boutique for an hour, just to check all was well and there were no problems that needed her attention. They had stopped for a while to feed the ducks on the pond, and now it was almost lunch time. Amy seemed fine. Heather had kept her at home as a precaution, but there had been no ill-effects, and her daughter was playing with her precious guinea pigs.

Going into her study, Heather watched from the window for a few moments, a sigh escaping unchecked. She wished Amy could have a more normal childhood, could make friends easily with other children, not always be so on her guard. The last two years had taken their toll on her daughter, just as they had on her. She hated that, hated to think that her own anxieties had transmitted themselves to Amy, had stripped the child of freedom and innocence. But things would get better. No matter how hard, she would see that Amy had a bright future, that she wanted for nothing.

Turning away, she checked her fax machine, pulling a handful of paper from the holding basket. She had not expected Murphy to work so quickly on this. Sitting down at her desk, she put the pages in order and began to check the information he had sent on Simon Clarke, trying to ignore the flicker of guilt she felt at the intrusion. But her state of mind, and any discreet violation of the man's privacy, were small prices to pay for Amy's well-being. She knew too well that she could not afford to take any chances.

From the first line, the details Murphy had uncovered were a surprise. His full name was Simon George Andrew Mortimer-Clarke. Thirty two years old, he was the only child of Lord George and Lady Ann Mortimer-Clarke of Stoneborough. Stoneborough House, Heather read, eyebrows rising, was a stately home set in huge parklands and woods in Derbyshire, not open to the public. Simon's father was an active member of the House of Lords.

Simon had been something of an embarrassment. Shunning the upper class existence, he had refused to shoot, to hunt, to keep up family tradition to enter the armed services, had shunned politics, and refused to use his full name. Instead of sitting at home as a privileged heir apparent, he had nurtured his sporting talent, representing his country at the decathlon at the highest level.

He had gone to university, taking a degree in sports science and teaching, at the same time maintaining his athletics. He had set new British and European records, had come close to a world record, and had been hailed as a great British hope for Olympic glory.

Amazed, Heather scanned the next sheet. His career had been shattered in a moment of pure, instinctive selflessness. One wet winter's day, six months before he went for gold at the Olympics, he had saved a child's life. He had thrown himself across an icy road, knocking the child out of the path of an oncoming, out-of-control lorry.

Heather bit her lip as she digested the details that followed. With no concern for his own safety, putting himself in mortal danger, he had sacrificed everything to save that little boy. He had taken the brunt of the impact as the lorry careered down the street, smashing into a parked car, knocking over a row of parking meters and crashing through a shop front. The driver had suffered a heart attack at the wheel, never to know the carnage he had unwittingly caused.

That only Simon had suffered major injuries had to be a miracle, Heather thought. His shoulder blade, joint and arm had been shattered, requiring several painful reconstructive surgeries. He had suffered broken ribs, a punctured lung, a fractured skull that led to a deep concussion, and several other minor cuts and knocks. According to the newspaper article Murphy had photocopied for her, it had taken months before Simon had been back on his feet again.

She tried to imagine what he had endured, not only in the physical sense but coming to terms with the ending of his career, of seeing all his hopes and dreams crumbling. It was something she understood, only too well. It also explained the wince he had been unable to conceal when Amy had knocked into him. Clearly, his injuries still troubled him despite the three years since the accident. No doubt about it, Simon Clarke, as he preferred to be known, was a very courageous man.

Heather skimmed through the rest of the report, the details of his involvement in saving the school, his new career, the hint of a broken engagement, the exasperation of his parents that he refused to return to the privileged fold of his family. Simon was his own man, choosing his own path. From all she had read, she could no longer doubt that he was a man she could trust, a man who could be trusted with Amy.

None of this meant she had to think about him all the time, Heather remonstrated with herself. She had satisfied herself about Simon's identity. That should be an end to it, but his image was fresh in her mind, his strong face, those incredible eyes, his flash of hostility and disapproval. She pushed the awareness aside. Neither Simon, nor any other man, was of interest to her, not any more. The lessons had been hard, but she had learned well.

Slipping the papers into a drawer and locking it, Heather stood up and walked through to the kitchen. She made some soup and Amy's favourite salad, then went to the back door to call her daughter in for lunch.

★　★　★

Following the afternoon's football training exercise with some of the older boys, Simon tidied up and made his way back across the sports' grounds to his office in the main building. Dusk was settling over the Sussex border country, an orange-red glow marking the last light of the setting sun away to the west. It was a beautiful place, a peaceful place, where a man could put his life back together. The office wing of the old house was quiet when he went in, quiet, but not lonely. It had an atmosphere, a comfortableness, about it, one that always helped to ease his frustrations, his inner concerns.

Hesitating at the doorway of the secretary's office, he stepped inside and ran through the card index she insisted on maintaining by hand. Finding the Marshall card, a frown creased his brow when he noted that only Heather Marshall was listed as Amy's next of kin, and as Ms, not Mrs. Considering the possibilities, he jotted down the address and telephone number on a piece of scrap paper, tapping it against his hand as he went down the passage to his own room.

Tonight he was dining out with friends. He still had an hour before he had to go upstairs to his flat on the top floor of the private wing, to shower and dress. He found himself staring at the phone number he had written down, temptation warring with commonsense. But it wouldn't hurt just to call and see how Amy was, he reasoned. If he satisfied himself everything was fine, it would be easier to put the little girl and her mother out of his mind.

Heather had just completed the

weekly accounts for the boutique when the telephone rang. Amy lay on the floor, working happily on an animal puzzle book. Setting down her pen and stretching stiff shoulders, Heather picked up the receiver before the answerphone cut in.

'Hello?'

'Ms Marshall? It's Simon Clarke.'

Hesitating, taken aback to hear his deep, warm voice, Heather ignored her quickening pulse and organised her thoughts.

'Yes, Mr Clarke?' she enquired coolly, trying to set aside the guilt she felt at reading the dossier Murphy had provided.

'I was just calling to see how Amy was doing.'

'Very well, thank you. There have been no after-effects, no problems. I'm sure she will be back at school on Monday.'

'I'm glad.'

'Thank you again for taking care of her.'

'My pleasure.'

After a brief pause, his voice changed, becoming warmer.

'She's a lovely little girl, and very brave.'

Heather smiled at her daughter who had sat up and was looking her.

'Mummy? Is that Simon?' Amy whispered, moving to her side.

When Heather nodded, the little girl gripped the phone cord.

'May I say hello?'

'Sorry, Mr Clarke,' Heather said. 'Amy is here. She wants to say hello.'

'Great.'

Heather heard the smile in his voice. Giving Amy the receiver, she leaned back in her chair and watched the animation on her daughter's face as she chatted to the man with whom she had built up such an instant rapport. She was amazed how comfortable Amy was. The child hated to talk on the telephone as a rule, would only speak to Heather's parents, with reluctance. Now she was giggling and talkative, giving the latest news in the lives of her precious guinea pigs.

'Will you come and visit me and see Ginger and Patch?'

Amy's invitation had Heather straightening in her chair. She placed her hand over her daughter's on the receiver, shaking her head.

'I'll ask Mummy. Just a minute.'

Heather covered the mouthpiece with her palm.

'Please can he come, Mummy? Please? He really wants to, and I never have anyone to see me. I want to show him the guinea pigs. Please?'

Heather bit her lip, cut to the quick by the loneliness so evident in her daughter's life. Was it her fault? She should try to encourage her to make more friends her own age, to open the house more to people. But it was hard to trust, and Amy had always been so shy, so reticent, until now. She looked down into that earnest little face and swallowed.

'Mr Clarke? About Amy's invitation . . . '

'I'd be glad to come,' he interjected, a hint of challenge in his voice.

'I see.'

Heather closed her eyes, wondering if her own anxiety, her own fear of her awareness of this man was making her unfair to her daughter. She smothered a worried sigh.

'How about Sunday afternoon?' Simon suggested now. 'About three?'

'All right, if you're sure.'

'I'll look forward to it, Ms Marshall.'

'So will Amy.'

'We'll see you on Sunday, then.'

Hanging up, she put her daughter out of her misery. Amy skipped round the room, clapping her hands in delight.

'Simon's coming to tea! Simon's coming to tea!' she chanted, a radiant gleam in her eyes.

It was a joy to see her daughter so happy, so looking forward to something, but she could not say the same for herself. She may have decided that

Simon Clarke was reliable and on the level, but that didn't mean she wanted him in her house. She didn't want any man in her house, not ever again. Filled with a sense of trepidation, for herself if not for Amy, Sunday loomed ahead of her casting a shadow on her thoughts.

4

He had to be insane, Simon grumbled to himself as he drove into the Surrey hills. The last thing he should be doing this damp, Sunday afternoon was going through with this visit to the Marshalls' home. He should never have agreed to Amy's suggestion, should have followed Heather's lead and made an excuse to refuse. But her cool, dismissive attitude had rankled with him. Perhaps he had accepted to spite her, perhaps because he was curious, perhaps because he had a genuine desire to see Amy and discover more about her home and background. What he did not want to consider was the possibility that it was Heather herself who drew him.

He thought back to Friday night when he had been out with friends for dinner. David and Ruth Collins were people who enjoyed his company for the person he was, not because they knew or cared about his background, his family, the wealth. They were also a couple who did not insist on trying to pair him off with one of their single, female friends. He could relax with them, feel at ease. It was during a lighthearted conversation after the meal, when David had been teasing his wife about her spending sprees and love of clothes, that Simon had remembered the school secretary's remarks about Heather Marshall.

'So, you frequent classy boutiques like 'Next to Nothing'?' he had asked with an air, he hoped, of casualness.

David had groaned and rolled his eyes in despair.

'Simon, please . . . '

'Take no notice.' Ruth had laughed. 'Yes, I shop there. Despite what he says, David loves the lacy lingerie I bring home, but it is fearfully expensive! Now what is your interest in a place like that, may I ask?'

Simon had managed to maintain a

cool unconcern.

'Someone at the school mentioned that one of the mothers owns it.'

'Really?' Ruth had exclaimed, intrigued. 'I've seen her, of course, Heather Marshall. A very beautiful woman still. Not that she's old. Mid-twenties, I imagine, but she's been retired for what, four years, more?'

'Retired?'

'Mm. She was a model, face on the cover of every magazine. You don't remember her?'

'No.'

'She gave it all up to get married. I don't remember the whole story now but there was some difficulty. Then she dropped out of sight. The boutique opened about eighteen months ago, all very discreet and low-profile.'

Now, as the entrance to the Marshalls' home came into view, Simon considered what his friends had told him. He wondered what difficulty Ruth had hinted at, what had happened in the lives of Heather and Amy Marshall.

And most of all, he wondered about Mr Marshall, husband and father.

Turning in between high brick walls, Simon drew the car up at the towering iron gates, a frown on his face. Opening the window, he pushed the entry button and waited for a response. The place was a fortress. He gazed at the gates, the security wire atop the walls, and wondered just whom the Marshalls were trying to keep out.

The intercom crackled, then Heather Marshall's voice greeted him.

'Yes? Who is it?'

'Simon Clarke.'

'Just a moment.'

He waited as a motor hummed and the gates swung open.

'Come on through, Mr Clarke.'

Raising his eyebrows, Simon put the car into gear and drove on, noticing in the rearview mirror that the gates glided shut behind him as soon as he had cleared them. His curiosity stirred once more as he drew up in front of the attractive, stone-built house and parked the car.

Unaccountably nervous, Heather wiped her hands on a tea towel and walked down the wide passage towards the front hall.

So, he had come. She had harboured the hope all over the weekend that he would cancel, or simply fail to arrive. She should have known better. Amy had been beside herself with excitement, and it had been Simon this and Simon that with such frequency that Heather thought she would scream.

Her daughter bounded in from the back garden, her face animated.

'Is it him? Is it him? Is Simon here?' she demanded, darting ahead towards the door.

'Yes, darling. Calm down!'

She opened the door and came face to face with Simon Clarke, handsome, imposing, intimidating. Having met him once, having thought about him far too often since, she should have been prepared for his impact on her, but she wasn't. For a tense, electric moment, their gazes locked, and Heather felt a heated anxiety mix with a blaze of unwanted feminine appreciation.

His eyes were even warmer than she remembered, their expression guarded yet curious, assessing yet admiring. Uncomfortable, Heather was relieved when Amy brushed past her and claimed Simon's attention.

Released from the pull of his gaze, she stepped back a pace inside the hall and watched him squat down to Amy's level. The child, though excited, was momentarily shy now that he was here, Heather saw. He handled it well, being friendly, accepting, without putting any pressure on. He ran the fingers of one hand through his dark hair, then his hand reached out to Amy, pretending to pluck something from behind her ear.

'What's this?' he asked with an exclamation of surprise, holding out the coin that now rested in his palm.

Amy giggled.

'How did you do that?'

'Magic!' He smiled, giving her the coin.

Clasping it in one hand, Amy slipped her other hand into his, her little fingers pale and lost against Simon's strength and tanned skin. Heather swallowed at the sight. It was a long time since Amy had interacted so freely with anyone, a long time since she had felt comfortable with a man, apart from her grandfather.

'Please,' Heather invited now, finding her manners and trying to hide her awkwardness, 'won't you come in?'

'Thanks.'

As he straightened and allowed Amy to lead him inside, Heather stepped back more sharply than she had intended, instinctively keeping a safe distance between them. Her gaze skittered nervously from his and she gestured down the passage.

'Amy, why don't you take Mr Clarke outside while I make some tea?'

'Come on,' Amy encouraged, tugging his hand. 'I've told Ginger and Patch that you're coming.'

As Simon walked away, an indulgent smile on his face, Heather closed the solid front door and leaned against it for a moment, one hand resting against her throat, feeling the dance of her pulse. There was nothing to get in such a tizzy about, she told herself, taking a calming breath. There was no reason Simon Clarke should alarm her, or pose any threat to her or her daughter. She knew that, and yet she felt a fear in a different kind of way, a fear that this man was stepping too intrusively into her thoughts and her life.

Collecting herself, she went through to the kitchen and put on the kettle, her gaze straying to the scene outside in the garden. She shook her head, a smile playing about her mouth as she saw Simon sitting on the ground nursing Amy, with a guinea pig on one arm, and holding the second pet in the other hand. He looked so natural, so patient, and Amy was animated, happy. The scene brought a lump to her throat. This was how it should be for the child.

This was the kind of life she had imagined for Amy, not one of secrecy, of hiding, of fear.

Turning away, blinking sudden tears from her eyes, Heather scooped tea into the pot and poured in the boiling water. For Amy's sake she would try her hardest to cope with this situation, but she hoped Simon Clarke would not stay long.

Outside, Amy was chattering away to Simon. He listened as she talked about her animals, his mind straying to his arrival at the house, lingering far longer than he wanted on Amy's mother. She was even more beautiful than he'd remembered. Dressed in a black dress, simple yet chic, her hair had been styled the same as before, its dark sheen shading one side of her face.

It was her eyes, however, that troubled him. The fear he had assumed was due to her concern over Amy was still there. Reserved, cool, nervous, she had maintained her distance. Was it a natural part of her character, this aloofness, or was it the result of something in her past? Enjoying the way Amy was opening up to him, her friendly chatter, her ease that he sensed was unusual for her, he refrained from making the cardinal error of asking the child about her father. It was clear that only she and her mother were at home. Just where was Mr Marshall, and what rôle did he play in the lives of these two wary, nervous females?

After staying with Amy for a while, he rose to his feet, dusting the damp grass from his trousers.

'I'll wander back to the kitchen, see if tea is ready,' he suggested as the child began to clean out the hutch.

'OK. You won't go, will you, before I've finished?'

'No, Amy, I'll be here when you're done.'

As he walked back to the house, he couldn't shake the feeling that for all it's charm, the house and grounds were like a luxurious prison.

He hesitated at the kitchen door, watching Heather Marshall for a moment, admiring her beauty, her poise. She affected him in a way he couldn't explain, a way he wanted to deny but was impossible to ignore. When she turned and saw him, her eyes widened in alarm. He did not enjoy the feeling that he frightened her in some way.

'Mr Clarke,' she murmured, her voice uneven, 'I didn't realise you were there.'

'Simon, please,' he invited with a smile.

Her answering smile was hesitant.

'As you wish. I'm Heather.'

She was too nervous, too edgy. He frowned.

'Amy will be in shortly,' he informed, keeping his voice light, studying her jerky movements as she set cups and saucers on the table and turned for a plate of cakes and biscuits. 'She's a delightful child.'

'Thank you.'

'I'm relieved to see no ill-effects from her fall.'

'No, she's fine.'

Her gaze made brief contact with his then flicked away as she glanced outside, keeping her daughter in sight.

'Please, sit down.'

Simon did as he was bid, resting his arms on top of the pine table. He felt ridiculously tongue-tied, and Heather didn't help. The keep-out vibes couldn't be more clear if they were written in letters and hung around her neck. Heather Marshall was not encouraging any polite approach.

'This is a nice house. Have you lived here long?' he asked, cursing his ham-fisted attempt to break the tense silence.

'About eighteen months.'

Simon nodded. That was about the same length of time she had owned the boutique, according to Ruth Collins. Another silence descended. He studied her as she kept herself occupied, a ruse, he was certain, to delay the time she would have to sit down over tea and talk to him.

He could well believe Ruth's claim that Heather Marshall had been a model, and he shared David's admiration. Her bone structure was classical, her mouth inviting, everything about her mysterious. He wished she would brush her hair back so he could see her whole face properly, her flawless complexion, those emotion-bruised eyes.

As she set a jug of milk on the table, he noticed for the first time that she wore a plain gold band on her ring finger. He had known she had to be married. He had no right to feel the burst of disappointment that curled through him and settled like a lead weight in his stomach. He should never have come here. Seeing Amy's guinea pigs had been an excuse, he admitted. He was drawn to the child, yes, wanted to understand her loneliness, to make a difference if he could. But it was Heather herself who had affected him in some way he could not understand.

Annoyed with himself, with the situation, with Heather for making him think and feel all kinds of things he didn't want to, his next question was voiced with an uncharacteristic lack of subtlety and finesse.

'Won't your husband be joining us?'

The instant the words left his mouth, he regretted them, regretted his tone, regretted most of all the effect the tactless words had on her. Every trace of colour drained from her face. She stared at him, eyes wide with pain and alarm, her hands shaking as they came to rest at her throat.

'I'm sorry, I — '

Simon stumbled to a halt, cursing his stupidity. He'd decided Mr Marshall had to be out on the golf course, away on business, but, what if she was a widow? He'd just put his foot in it in a monumental way. Concerned, he rose to his feet, wanting to ease the distress he had so clearly caused her. He took a step towards her, halting uncertainly when he saw the dart of fear in her eyes. She felt threatened by him. Something tightened inside him like a fist, cold, hard, painful.

Still pale, her head bent, the fall of hair hiding her pained expression, she sat in a chair at the table, seeming to him small and vulnerable despite her height and grace. When she spoke, her voice was husky with pain, the words laced with confusion and anxiety.

'Why have you come here? What do you want? What do you know of James Marshall?'

'Heather, I'm sorry. I know nothing about your husband. I had no right to ask, no right to be curious. I have no ulterior motives. Please accept my apology for being so rude and ungracious.'

Conscious of Simon returning to his seat opposite her, Heather tried to rein in her wild thoughts and calm the frantic thud of her heart. His apology had been sincere. He couldn't know the facts. Of course he couldn't know, just as there was no way he could understand what chaos his thoughtless question had caused in her mind, the sudden panic, the rush of agonising memories that flooded through her.

Unable to meet his gaze, she linked her icy fingers together, the knuckles whitening under the strain, and forced herself to calm down. She could not go on letting every passing comment have this effect on her. She could not go on imagining ulterior motives lay behind every unwanted enquiry. If she hoped to give Amy any kind of a normal life, she had to find a way to cope, even if she could never come to terms.

She wondered if Simon recognised her from the minor fame she had endured in the past. He had given no indication of knowing who she was. She hoped to keep it that way. On top of her concern, she again felt a twinge of guilt at the knowledge she had gained about him. She felt awkward, uncertain what to say to him. Somehow she had to behave with cool politeness until this afternoon was over.

'Darling, there you are,' she exclaimed with relief as Amy appeared at the back door. 'Wash your hands, and we'll have some tea.'

Rising to her feet, she lifted her daughter to the sink. She was conscious of Simon's gaze on them. It sent a tingle up her spine. Her hands dried, Amy clambered on to a chair next to Simon and chattered to him as Heather poured the tea and passed round cake and biscuits.

'Milk, please, no sugar,' Simon responded to her enquiring glance.

Heather passed him a cup and saucer, then filled a glass with cold milk for Amy. Finally, she poured her own tea and sat down. Opposite him, she was subjected to the full force of his gaze. Her eyes locked with his, and she found herself unable to look away.

There was concern in the dark depths, concern for her, regret that he had been the cause of her anxiety. But there was also the interest any man would have in an attractive woman.

Heather had sought to avoid the interest of any man, but Simon Clarke was an impossible man to ignore. Inside, hidden away in some locked and forgotten part of her, a part she had imagined buried for ever, an answering flicker of interest began to glow. The realisation of it made her more anxious and nervous than ever.

It was fortunate, Heather decided, that her normally reticent daughter should be monopolising the conversation. She had no idea what she would have said otherwise. She could hardly ask about his family, his background, his accident. That would display a knowledge, an interest, she was not yet ready to reveal. Sipping her tea, she watched him with Amy.

He listened to the child, encouraged her, drew her out of herself in a way no-one else ever had. Heather marvelled at it, yet at the same time, she felt confused, uneasy, almost resentful. She had been protective of Amy for so long, it was difficult to let anyone, especially this disturbing man who was still a stranger, get too close.

'Mummy, can Simon have some more cake?'

Heather couldn't help but smile at Amy's cunning.

'I'm sure Simon can have a piece if he wants one,' she teased, knowing Amy was desperate for another piece herself!

She caught Simon's gaze, reading his amusement at Amy's ploy.

'Simon's had more than enough,' he said, 'and it was delicious. I can't remember when I last had home-made cake.'

'I'm glad you liked it.'

Heather's gaze lingered on him for a moment, then she looked back at Amy who shifted restlessly on her seat. Innocently, she smiled at the child.

'Would you like another slice, Amy?'

'Yes, please!'

She waited for the plate to be passed, then helped herself to the largest, stickiest piece. Taking a huge bite, she met Heather's gaze, tried an apologetic smile and murmured, with her mouth full, 'Thank you.'

Simon's eyes shone with laughter and Heather felt herself responding to him. After sharing a gaze that left her feeling at once drawn to him and yet painfully nervous, Heather cleared her throat.

'More tea?' she asked nervously.

'Thanks.'

His fingers brushed hers as she passed a full cup back to him, their touch sending a tingle of awareness up her arm. Feeling foolish and uncertain, she concentrated on Amy who had finished her cake in record time.

'No, young lady,' she stressed, forestalling her daughter's imminent desire for yet another slice. 'I think you've had quite enough.'

'But . . . '

'Have you got hollow legs?' Simon asked, diverting Amy's protest by tickling her.

'Don't be silly,' she said. 'No-one has hollow legs!'

'They don't?' he asked, disappointment on his face.

' 'Course not. Legs have got bones in,' Amy scoffed.

Simon's eyebrows rose.

'Then where would you put more cake?'

'In my tummy.'

'But it's such a little tummy,' he teased. 'Now,' he said, scooping Amy off the chair and setting her on her feet on the floor, 'I'd better come and say goodbye to Patch and Ginger, and then it'll be time for me to go.'

The cake forgotten, clasping his hand and clearly disappointed he would soon leave, Amy led Simon from the kitchen. Heather watched them go, a funny little knot tightening in her chest. She cleared the table, and was setting the washed cups, saucers and plates on the drainer when they returned from the garden.

Amy looked sorrowful now that the afternoon was coming to a close. Heather smiled her understanding.

'Simon's going now,' the child said sadly.

'You've had a nice time, haven't you?' Heather asked.

Amy nodded vigorously.

'And have you thanked him for coming?'

Amy, pulling on Simon's shirt, drew him down for a hug.

'Thank you. I'm glad you came.'

'So am I, poppet.'

'Will you come for tea again?' the child begged.

Heather met Simon's gaze over Amy's head, her breath catching in her throat.

'We'll have to see,' he murmured after a moment, taking the small hand in his and walking down the passage to the front door. 'Thanks for the tea, Heather.'

'You're welcome,' she responded, opening the door. 'Thank you for making Amy's afternoon.'

'No problem.'

When he extended his hand, Heather

accepted the gesture, reluctantly subjecting herself to his disturbing touch. His fingers closed around hers, warm, strong. A shiver ran through her. She was disturbed both by Simon, and by her memories.

'You take care now,' Simon instructed as he released her hand and turned to Amy. 'We'll look forward to seeing you back at school next week.'

Heather gathered Amy close, her hands resting on her thin shoulders. Together they stood by the front door as Simon crossed to his car. Returning his wave, Heather watched as he drove down the drive in the gathering dusk. Stepping inside, she pressed the switch to open the gates, careful to close them again as soon as the rear lights of his car disappeared.

Sensing Amy's deflated mood, she drew the child inside and shut the door. Taking her hand, she led her back to the kitchen and set some paper and crayons on the table.

'Why don't you draw Simon a nice

picture of your afternoon?' she suggested, pleased when Amy smiled her enthusiasm at the idea.

With her daughter occupied, Heather found she had too much time to think. The most worrying thing of all was that all the thoughts centred around the imposing, and far too attractive, Simon Clarke.

After school the next day, Simon tried to convince himself that it was mere coincidence that he happened to be loitering in the driveway as the day pupils made their way home. He was talking to a group of children, a couple of whom he believed had the potential of being excellent middle-distance runners, as they waited for their minibus.

As the minibus rounded the curve in the sweeping drive, the children gathered up their belongings. Their farewells ringing in his ears, Simon turned back to the main building, sauntering across the grass in time to see Heather and Amy leave the junior wing. Pausing mid stride, he watched them. Heather looked as chic and graceful as he had come to expect. Bundled in a charcoal coat against the stiff autumn breeze, her hair was restrained by an elegant scarf she had tied below her chin.

By her side, Amy looked small and vulnerable, a tenseness evident even at this distance. He wondered if school always made her so unhappy. Saddened by the thought of her lack of ease and the absence of friends her own age, Simon walked on slowly towards the parked cars.

'Simon!'

He smiled at Amy's excited shout, touched by the way her face brightened when she saw him. The same could not be said of Heather, he noted. He had spent the last twenty-four hours thinking about her, about her fear, her aloofness, her unease. None of his questions found answers. There were only more questions still about this beautiful, enigmatic woman.

'Hello, Amy,' he greeted, ignoring the ache in his shoulder as he scooped Amy up in his arms. 'How are you? Did you do some nice things in class?'

A faint pout marred Amy's countenance.

'We did some sums and some writing and some reading.'

'Don't you like doing that?' he asked, his gaze straying to Heather who waited at the car.

'It's all right, I suppose. I don't like having to read in front of the others.'

Simon imagined it would be an ordeal for this shy, little girl, already feeling she was apart from her classmates. He wished he could help her, wished he could unravel her secrets. Setting her back on her feet, his hand unconsciously rubbing his shoulder, he walked with her back to her mother.

'Hello, Heather.'

'Simon,' she said politely.

'Mummy, can I get my picture from the car?'

'Of course, darling.'

Simon watched as Heather dragged her gaze away and fumbled with the car keys. Reaching inside, she drew a sheet of paper from the parcel shelf and handed it to the excited child.

'Here, Simon,' Amy offered, holding out the paper. 'I drew this for you to thank you for coming yesterday.'

He looked at the scene, two figures in the garden with the guinea pigs, and off to the side, three figures sitting down to tea. It looked cosy, homely, symbolic of something wistful and desired that Amy did not have. It brought a lump to his throat.

Raising his gaze, he met the cool, unfathomable hazel of Heather's eyes. They were clouded now, anxious, pained. Suddenly, Simon wanted to take that pain away. Just once he wanted to see her with laughter in those eyes, happiness on her face, wanted to banish the fear that seemed to plague her. Why was she so afraid? And why had she reacted as she had when he had mentioned her husband so clumsily the day before?

'Thank you, Amy,' he said, pulling his

attention away from Heather and conjuring up a smile for the little girl. 'It's a lovely drawing. I'll put it on the wall in my kitchen.'

As Amy beamed her pleasure, Heather opened the car door.

'Come on, darling, I'm sure Simon has plenty to do, and we must be getting home.'

'All right.'

Simon smiled at Amy's woebegone expression.

'Cheer up, Amy. I'll see you again soon.'

'Tomorrow?' she enthused.

'We'll see.'

Amy sucked her thumb, hesitating again before complying with her mother's request.

'Will you be coming next week?'

'Next week?'

Simon looked at Heather and raised an eyebrow.

'Did I miss something?'

Tucking some stray wisps of hair back beneath her scarf, Heather shook her head as she replied, 'Amy has a school trip arranged for next week and she's a bit reluctant about it.'

'You are?'

Simon squatted down to Amy's level.

'Why don't you want to go?'

The child shrugged.

'Where are you going?'

'An outdoor museum.'

'Ah, at Singleton. It's lovely there. They have horses, pigs, other animals, and a big pond with lots of ducks.'

Amy brightened.

'They do?'

'Yes. Is Mummy going with you?'

He glanced up and intercepted Heather's nod of confirmation.

'Well then, what have you to worry about? It'll be fun.'

'Are you going to come, too?'

'I don't know,' he replied, taken aback. 'I'll see how busy I am.'

'Please?'

'Amy,' Heather chided. 'That's enough. I'm sorry, Simon.'

He straightened and smiled.

'That's OK. Don't worry about it. I'm flattered to be asked. I'll see what I can do, Amy. See you soon.'

As he stood, hands in his pockets, and watched them drive away, Simon told himself the idea of going on the school trip appealed to him because he loved the Downlands Open Air Museum, and also because he was touched that Amy wanted his company. That he was drawn most of all by the prospect of spending some time with Heather was an alarming possibility he thrust to the back of his mind.

Heather herself could not explain the nervous tension that tightened her insides as she drove home from the school. Simon had been framed in the rearview mirror as she had driven down the drive, an imposing, disturbing figure. She could have died when Amy had nagged him about joining them on the trip. The thought of being thrown into his company for the duration of the outing made her unaccountably anxious. He was a busy man, with classes and responsibilities of his own. He was being polite and kind to Amy.

He wouldn't come, she convinced herself . . . or would he?

5

Heather's week-long hope that Simon would be unable to join the outing to the museum was dashed as soon as she pulled the car to a stop outside the school. The coach that would transport the twenty or so children, assorted parents, and the class teacher, Joan Jeffries, was standing in the driveway, the engine running. Beside the open door, ticking off the children's names as they entered the coach, was Simon Clarke.

Amy let out an excited cry when she spotted him, struggling with her small rucksack as she slid from the car.

'I knew he would go with us, Mummy!' she called out happily before turning to trot across the grass towards him.

Her heart sinking, Heather took her own bag, locked the car, and followed at a more sedate pace. She watched as Amy tugged his sleeve and he looked down with a smile, his free hand ruffling her hair. He helped the child up the step, pointed at something and made her laugh as he bent to whisper in her ear.

' 'Morning,' Simon greeted her as he stepped back outside the door, his eyes steady, warm, disturbing as they looked into hers.

Heather nodded her own greeting, trying to appear calmer than she felt.

'Good morning.'

Trying to hide the unconscious flinch when his hand rested on her arm to guide her up the steps, Heather bit her lip and allowed a small sigh of relief when new arrivals claimed his attention. She found Amy perched excitedly on one of the seats, her nose pressed up to the window. Unhooking the strap of her shoulder bag, Heather slid in next to her daughter.

'Simon saved the seats for us,' Amy beamed, turning to her, and her voice dropped to a conspiratorial whisper. 'He said not to tell anyone that he was playing truant for the day.'

Heather smiled, amazed anew at the difference Simon's presence could make to her child's nature. Only that morning, Amy had dallied over her breakfast, uncertain and nervous at the planned trip with her classmates. Even Heather's presence had not evoked such enthusiasm.

Now that they were here, her own nervous uncertainty was returning with a vengeance. She so wanted Amy to enjoy the day, to begin relating to her classmates. Simon's presence could help, and anything that helped Amy was welcome. It was her own reaction to the man that worried her.

The last of the party accounted for, Joan Jeffries and Simon climbed aboard and closed the door. The class teacher took the window seat across the centre aisle from Heather, and Simon the one next to her. Even with the width of the aisle between them,

Heather felt his nearness.

Casting a sidelong glance at him while he discussed something with Joan, Heather surreptitiously studied his appearance. The dark hair was ruffled, rakish, the low autumn sunlight streaming through the windows and bringing out some reddish tints. He was wearing casual but smart brown trousers. Over his cream sweater he wore a brown leather jacket.

When Simon stopped talking and had turned to look at her, she was embarrassed. Startled, her gaze locked with his. His eyes were filled with a mix of interest, curiosity and appreciation. All made Heather nervous.

'You said you had been to Singleton before,' she said, searching for some safe topic of conversation.

'Yes, many times. Aside from the work that it does, there is just something so tranquil and timeless about the place that it keeps drawing me back. Have you never been?'

'No. No, I haven't.'

Despite living on the county border for eighteen months, she and Amy had explored very few of the attractions that the area had to offer, Heather admitted to herself. What with school, the boutique, the move and other things, she allowed with a frown, there had been little in the way of outings together. She would make an effort to rectify that. Perhaps today would be a good start.

Aware that Simon was watching her, she made an effort to banish her thoughts, and summoned a smile. She was saved from further comment as Amy leaned over her lap as far as the seat-belt would allow, and drew Simon's attention. Absently her fingers stroked Amy's soft strands of hair. As he encouraged the child to chat and ask questions about their destination, Heather looked out of the window at the changing countryside that basked in the late sunshine.

The journey over, the driver turned the coach into the carpark of the museum that nestled in a hollow at the foot of the South Downs, north of Chichester. The noisy group of children disembarked and were encouraged into an orderly line. Amy hung near the back, unwilling to let either Heather or Simon out of her sight.

Heather noticed how Amy mixed with the others with reluctance. She was ill at ease. Heather glanced at Simon who walked by her side.

'I wish she would make friends,' Heather murmured her concern. 'I hate to see her lonely, shunning the other children.'

'Has she been like that since she was tiny?'

Simon's question made her pause. What could she say? She had no wish to divulge their past to anyone, could not bring herself to open up and explain the reasons for Amy's behaviour, the reasons, too, for her own anxiety and loneliness, and she was lonely, Heather realised, an ache in her heart. Just like Amy, she was starved of the companionship of people her own age. It was her own doing, but it ached nonetheless.

'What's wrong?'

She blinked and focused on the concern that darkened Simon's eyes.

'Nothing,' she protested, attempting a smile.

As she spun away from him, intending to catch up with the line of children snaking ahead, her bag slid down her arm. Instinctively, Simon reached out to save it. Instinctively, Heather shrunk from him.

'Don't touch me,' she protested before she could stop herself.

She heard Simon mutter a curse under his breath, and watched as he backed off a step, giving her room. The threat of tears pricked her eyes, despair at her unbidden response. Was it always going to be like this? For ever? As she lowered her gaze from the frowning dawn of understanding in his eyes, a breeze rolled down the hills and blew her hair back from her face.

The indrawn breath she heard could have been a trick of the wind in the trees, but Heather recognised the sound for what it was. She knew that it was Simon's reaction, and she knew that he had seen. As Heather fumbled in her bag and drew out a silk scarf, fastening it over her billowing hair and tying it under her chin, Simon struggled to contain his rage. The signs had been there. He had known something was wrong, not just in Amy's past but in Heather's.

He had suspected something, had not known what, not until an unpleasant seed had begun to germinate when she had flinched from his touch for the second time that day. But it had been during those seconds when the wind had blown back her hair which she wore curled across her cheek and down her throat that the horrifying realisation had slammed home. Someone, and he could only assume it was her husband, had injured her. He forced his gaze away from her, forced himself to act naturally. Jamming his hands in his pockets, he gave her the space she needed and walked at her side down towards the children and adults clustered round the small square.

The make-up he'd spotted had been good, shading the scars. He dreaded to imagine what had caused them, what they were like without their skilfully-applied covering. He had never been a violent person, but had James Marshall been within reach at that moment, Simon did not like to consider what he may have done. All he could feel through his own anger, was Heather's pain. How could anyone do this to her?

He wanted to hold her, to comfort her, but he understood that for now, at least, touching was out of the question. If he hoped to be anything at all in Heather's life, and he was coming to realise just how much he wanted that, he had to play this carefully. He could not run the risk of scaring her any more than she was already. However long it took, whatever he had to do, he would work to earn her trust.

Damping down his own emotions, trying to formulate some ideas on how he could begin to encourage Heather to confide in him, Simon spent much of the morning trailing round the exhibits behind the children, lost in thought. When they arrived back at the main section of the museum, it was time for lunch. Their party divided up into groups, some selecting picnic tables near the large mill pond, but Simon chose to accompany Amy, Heather and a couple of others to sit in the sun near a large tree.

Conscious of Heather's unease, he sat down, keeping Amy between them. The little girl responded to his questions about the things they had seen, and it was no surprise to him that she had been most taken with the animals. Smiling at Amy, he leaned back on his elbows on the blanket, stretching his long legs out in front of him, shifting to find a comfortable position that did not put undue strain on his shoulder.

'See that cottage?' he asked, nodding in the direction of one of the buildings that had been renovated and assembled on the site.

Amy followed his gaze and nodded.

'It's my favourite.'

'Mine, too. I always think I would love to live in it, but life must have been very hard for the people back then.'

'Mrs Jeffries said they didn't have proper lights or radiators or water,' Amy said, munching a sandwich.

'Or television,' he agreed gravely, smiling at Amy's look of horror.

Simon glanced across at Heather. She looked tense, he thought, wishing he could put her at ease. He realised now that he was not the only one she was distant with, scared of. Tall and elegant though she was, she looked somehow small and fragile, too, and he ached for her.

As if sensing his thoughts, she raised her head and looked at him, the shadows that gave a haunted look to her eyes touching his heart. Somehow, he determined, he would show her that life could be good and happy, that she did not have to be afraid any more.

Unable to look away from the intensity of Simon's gaze, Heather recognised the understanding in his eyes and was thankful there was no pity, only a banked anger on her behalf. When Amy, her lunch finished, announced her intention to search for conkers, Heather felt as nervous as a teenager at being left with Simon. There were others nearby, but far enough away that Amy's departure gave them sufficient privacy not to be overheard.

Heather was unsure if she wanted to talk. She never spoke about her scars, both physical ones and mental. Even more, she never talked about what, or who, had caused them.

'It's pretty here,' she said after a while, her voice more husky than usual as she broke the silence that had settled between them.

Simon nodded.

'I never know if it's the setting, the history, the timelessness, or the general atmosphere, but it always makes me feel peaceful. Can we talk?'

His question, softly voiced, serious and intent, made her sigh.

'I don't know.'

She looked up at him, met the sincerity in his eyes, the desire for knowledge and understanding, and the underlying flare of anger on her behalf.

'I don't talk about — er — things, very often.'

'Ever?'

Heather looked away.

'Never,' she admitted.

Beside her, she sensed him moving. He was careful to keep a distance between them, she noticed, touched by his sensitivity to her feelings.

'Can I ask you one thing?'

'Yes,' she agreed, responding to the concern in his voice.

'About Amy,' he began, pausing as if searching for the right way to phrase his question. 'Did anything happen to Amy?'

Heather suppressed a shiver.

'No, Simon, but she saw, and something else happened that frightened her. She was young, but she remembers.'

And so do I, she added silently, biting her lip. Every day I remember. She heard Simon expel a shaky breath. He had turned on to his side, facing her, his head propped in one hand.

'This,' she whispered, gesturing nervously towards her face, 'was an accident. It just happened the once.'

'Once was too much. What happened, Heather?' he asked, controlling the threat of anger in his voice.

For several moments she didn't speak. Collating her thoughts, she looked towards her daughter, seeing that another little girl from her class had joined her in the search for conkers. Amy appeared uncertain, painfully shy. Heather ached for her.

Then Amy summoned a smile and

shared her haul with her new friend. The other child's pleasure and happy chatter somehow seemed to penetrate Amy's reserve, and with an expression of surprise she made the first overtures of friendship. Heather was thrilled. She knew how difficult it was for Amy to accept people. If her little daughter could be brave enough to overcome her anxieties and shyness and reach out for a new friendship, couldn't she do the same?

Her gaze swung back to Simon. She found that he watched her, waiting with silent patience, seemingly aware of the inner battle that raged inside her, and allowing her time to reconcile it. He was offering her the opportunity to expunge the pain that festered within her. By doing so, could she unlock the inner door that was preventing her getting on with her life? It would be difficult. It would hurt, but if she wanted to help Amy enjoy a bright future, she herself had to come to terms with the past.

Was she brave enough to take that step?

Heather was relieved she did not have to find the answer to her own question straight away. While she was still pondering her options, fighting both her inner fear and the unusual urge to confide in Simon, the class teacher returned, shepherding the rest of the children and parents together.

She was amazed how Amy blossomed that afternoon. It seemed that her tentative efforts at the first real friendship of her life had done wonders for her confidence. Under Simon's guidance, she took an active interest in all that went on, and Heather was grateful that Simon made sure to include Amy's new friend, Jilly Walker, in whatever else they were doing. She didn't know how she could ever thank Simon for his perceptiveness.

Feeling almost in awe of her daughter's bravery that day, Heather felt she had to make some kind of gesture of her own. Back at the school, while Amy was gathering her belongings and saying goodbye to Jilly, Heather turned to Simon.

'Thank you for today. I can't believe the change in Amy,' she confided, wishing her voice did not sound quite so breathless and throaty. 'Simon, about earlier. I was wondering, if you had time, if you'd like to stop by the house at the weekend? Only it's Amy's birthday. My parents are taking her to a Disney film in the afternoon, then I was planning to have a special tea. I'm sure she would like you to come.'

'I'd love to. What time?'

Heather made an effort to control her nervous gesture of lacing her fingers together, but she could not help but be nervous when he looked at her that way. She cleared her throat.

'If you came about four on Saturday?'

His slow smile warmed her from the inside out.

'Four would be fine.'

An excursion to a large toy shop in the nearby town furnished Simon with the presents he wanted for Amy's birthday. He smiled at the sight of the parcels on the car seat beside him, especially the life-size cuddly black puppy that peeped out of the carrier bag, a mischievous look on its face.

He knew it would take time for the changes that had begun in Amy at the museum the other afternoon to come to fruition, but already he could see what a bright and lively little girl lurked beneath the reserved, anxious exterior. Not for the first time, he wondered what kind of woman Heather could be if she could be coaxed out of her protective shell. He would only hope that this invitation would be a start for Heather to break free of her past as Amy had begun to do.

Simon steered the car down the narrow, hilly lanes. Was he getting in too deep with Heather and her daughter? He had never meant it to happen, but he cared. He could not hide the truth from himself. More than anything, he wanted to ease the hurt, wanted to see Heather smile, to see that fear and pain vanish from her dark eyes. As he pulled up at their security gate, he wondered why he should imagine he could help anyone else when his own emotions about his past were in such a mess.

'Oh, blast!' Heather muttered when the entry phone sounded on the dot of four o'clock.

What was she doing? Why had she asked him here? How could she even think of discussing her past, opening up the hurt again? She used the couple of minutes it took for him to drive in, gather his packages and arrive at the front door to try and compose herself. That composure almost evaporated at the sight of him, imposing, handsome. Unconsciously, she stepped back as he entered the house, keeping that invisible distance between them, a distance no-one had been allowed to cross in a long time.

'Simon, you shouldn't have brought all this!' she exclaimed as she was diverted by all his gifts.

'It's just a few books and a cuddly toy,' he said light-heartedly.

'Amy will love them. My parents haven't brought her back yet, but they should be here soon. I was just finishing decorating her cake in the kitchen. Would you like to come through?'

He nodded and followed her to the kitchen. After he had deposited his packages on a spare length of worktop, he sat at the table, watching her as she put the final touches to the birthday cake.

'There, what do you think?' she asked, turning her creation round for him to see.

'It's wonderful! The guinea pigs are perfect. And what else have you got on here? Horses, sheep, pigs, the animals from the museum? However have you done this in the time?'

Warmed by his obvious approval, Heather smiled again.

'Only by burning the midnight oil,' she confessed. 'It was the only time I could work on it without a certain nosey parker spoiling the surprise!'

She cleared the mess away and laid the table for the birthday tea, knowing she was keeping herself busy to put off the inevitable time when she would have to face him.

'Shall we go through to the sitting-room?' she asked at length, hating the nervous waver in her voice.

At his agreement, she led him back down the hall and into the sun-filled room that looked out on the garden. Anxious, she walked towards the windows, keeping her back to him. This was going to be more difficult than she'd imagined. Perhaps she was not as brave as Amy after all.

'Heather?'

She turned at the sound of his voice, heard the questioning note that mixed with the warm understanding.

'Yes?'

'We don't have to do this,' he told her, eyes filled with concern. 'If you want to talk, I want to listen, but only if you are ready, if it's what you want.'

With a stiff nod, she wrapped her arms around herself, glancing at the carriage clock on the mantle. She had expected Amy before this. A small shiver of alarm ran through her, but she forced it away. She could not allow herself to get panicky every time her daughter was out of her sight. Once more her gaze slid to Simon, and she crossed the room to sit facing him.

'This is so hard. I've never talked about things before, not even with my parents.'

'Keeping it bottled up inside doesn't help, Heather.'

'I know, but that doesn't make it easier.'

She wondered briefly if he was speaking from personal experience, if he had expunged the horror he had been through himself by talking to friends and family. Or was he like her? Had he closed in on himself as a way of coping with the physical and mental pain? Was that why he had recognised her own and Amy's anxieties with such accuracy?

His eyes were clear, their expression patient, and Heather felt a need she had never experienced before to share her past with this man. It frightened her, because she recognised that Simon Clarke was coming to be far too important in her life. She was not ready for that — maybe she never would be. But unless she took the first step she wouldn't know.

'My parents were never well off. They struggled to give me things — a good education, a better life than they'd had,' Heather began.

She watched as Simon leaned back on the sofa, relaxed and unthreatening, encouraging her to continue with a supportive smile.

'I don't want to imply that they ever exploited me,' she hastened to explain, 'but when I was in my early teens, my mother took me along to a department store for an audition to model a new line of clothes. It was an adventure, something different, but I never minded whether I was successful or not. Then I was chosen, and that was the start of it. My parents invested my earnings for my future, and some was used to improve our day-to-day living. By the time I left school, I was earning more than I could have imagined, and instead of going on to college and university, as I had intended, my parents encouraged me to make the most of my success.'

She paused and frowned, never comfortable that others found her looks so appealing.

'I must admit it was with some reluctance that I shelved half-formed ideas of a career in law to concentrate on modelling.'

Heather glanced at him, buoyed by the warm understanding in his eyes.

'It was not at all glamorous like people think. It was hard work, often boring, but I went along with it because it was familiar, something I could do, something that paid well and allowed me to give something back to my parents who had made so many sacrifices for me. I guess that sounds noble, or crazy.'

She laughed self-consciously.

'Anyway, I was on a fashion shoot in Edinburgh when I met James Marshall. He was a journalist, doing an assignment for a magazine on the photographer. We talked, commented on the fact that we had the same surname, and when he asked me to join him for dinner at the hotel, I accepted.'

Simon watched her as she talked, seeing all the emotions play across her face, relieved she was talking, but conscious of the weight of dread settling cold and heavy in his stomach.

'Everything was fine in the beginning,' she went on, her gaze sliding from his, her fingers knotting in her lap, displaying her tension. 'I was flattered that someone older and sophisticated was interested in me. I'd never had a steady boyfriend before. There was never time between school and modelling assignments. I was lonely. I was eighteen by then, with no close friends, and my mother was unwell and no longer came on every trip with me. I was swept off my feet, incredibly foolish. But then hindsight is a wonderful thing, isn't it?'

Sensing the question was rhetorical, Simon maintained his silence, unwilling to halt her flow of words.

'My parents were not at all keen on James, but I wouldn't listen to them, or to my agent. I was sure it was true love, that I should follow my heart. How stupid I was.'

The words were laced with a bitter pain that turned his blood cold.

'What happened, Heather?'

'Oh, I married him, fool that I was.'

She rose to her feet with a burst of suppressed energy and began to pace the room. He wanted to go to her, to reassure her, to ease her pain, but he knew that he couldn't, not yet.

'I never realised how obsessive he was until it was too late. It began before we had even returned from our honeymoon. He would make a comment about what I was wearing, that it was too revealing or enticing. Then he would challenge me, accuse me of looking at another man. It just wasn't true. It went on from there, steadily worse and worse. Looking back I can see I should have admitted at the beginning I had made a mistake, but a combination of pride and naïveté kept me there.'

Simon hated to hear the recrimination in her voice. He watched, frowning, as he realised she blamed herself and not James Marshall. With a small shake of her head, she walked to the window and gazed out at the dusk-shadowed garden.

'I didn't quite reach supermodel status, but I had a cosmetics contract and advertised a perfume on television. I had the fashion work, and I travelled all over the world. James knew all that I did when we met, but he couldn't handle the attention I received. Professional attention,' she added, as if the distinction were necessary.

'You are a beautiful woman. In the public eye, you were bound to attract attention. Isn't that why designers and manufacturers wanted you to be seen in their creations?'

'Of course.' She shrugged, shoulders stiff. 'I just found it hard to see myself that way. To me it was a job, nothing more.'

He wished he could remember her from a few years ago, but he had concentrated on his athletics to the exclusion of all else. He had lived and breathed his sport, training almost obsessively to achieve his dreams, dreams that had been shattered in minutes that fateful day. Dragging his mind back to Heather, his gaze rested on her and she turned to lean against the windowsill, her hands rubbing up and down her arms.

'Perceived beauty can be an affliction, Simon,' she finally responded. 'To James I was deliberately inciting, enticing men. He was jealous, frighteningly jealous. He made accusations, followed me, systematically twisted things to undermine my self-worth and destroy my self-esteem.'

She paused and sucked in a breath.

'The worst of it was that I allowed him to do it.'

'You are not suggesting you blame yourself?' he asked incredulously.

A silence descended, charging the room with tension. When she lowered her gaze, Simon felt a welling of anger at what her husband had done to her.

'Heather, the man mentally abused you.'

She stiffened at his words, but made no response. Frustrated, Simon allowed her to continue her story.

'When Amy was born,' Heather went on, walking back to the chair she had recently vacated, 'I gave up work. For a while things settled down, but after a few months, it began again. If I so much as smiled at someone else, talked to another man, James saw ulterior motives, sinister goings-on. He humiliated me in public, told me what a useless mother I was, that kind of thing. There were excuses, of course. He told me he was under pressure at work, that his problems all stemmed from me, that my ineptitude, my imagined faithlessness were to blame.'

Simon wanted to demand why she hadn't left him, why she hadn't taken Amy and returned to her parents, but he knew that was unfair. He could only imagine how Heather must have felt being subjected to the bully tactics of her husband. It must have seemed to her that there was no way out. And if she had come to feel that she was responsible . . .

'How did you manage to get free of him?' he asked now, keeping the anger he felt from his voice with difficulty.

Heather shivered, her gaze rising to meet his.

'I nearly didn't, Simon. What happened next was the biggest nightmare of my life.'

6

Rising to her feet, she paced the room, giving herself a few moments to compose her thoughts before she could contemplate revealing to him the trauma that had occurred with James. She frowned when she saw how dark it was outside. Lingering to close the curtains she turned back to Simon and glanced at her watch.

'What time do you make it?' she asked.

He checked his own watch, surprise on his face.

'A little after five thirty,' he confirmed.

'They should have been back by now.'

'I'm sure they are fine. The traffic is probably bad in town.'

A tense silence stretched between them. Heather continued to pace, distracted by her thoughts, her fear for her daughter's well-being increasing. No matter how she tried to convince herself that it was the memories roused by talking to Simon of her past that were making her edgy, her unease remained.

Simon watched in silence as she paced the room. He wanted to bring new happiness to Heather's life. His feelings surprised and troubled him. Could he, who had so nearly given up on himself in his darkest moments, teach this woman how to love and trust and laugh again? In so many ways they were similar. They both had a past to overcome, both had dreams shattered by fate. But immersing himself in Heather's and Amy's lives had made a difference to his own thinking.

Absently, he raised a hand to knead the ache in his shoulder. Perhaps it was time he confided in her about his own demons. He wanted to hold her, to comfort her, but he didn't dare, not until she had learned she could trust him. He understood about trust, about how hard it was. Before the accident he had been free with his trust, and his love, but he had learned then that nothing came without its cost. A coldness settled inside him as thoughts turned to Eileen.

'I can't stay with you now, Simon. I can't handle it. I'm sure you understand,' she had announced following the aftermath of his accident.

The words were clear even now, as vivid as they had been when he had lain in the hospital bed and watched the beautiful, heartless Eileen return his engagement ring, looking at him as if he were flawed, somehow contemptible in her eyes.

She had taken one look at his battered body, learned he would never be what he had once been, and then she had made her choice, had thrown his love back at him with his ring, completing the losses he had had to endure.

'It was never me you wanted, was it,

Eileen? What was it, my family's money, my inherited name?'

Her silence had spoken volumes.

'Goodbye, Eileen.'

He recalled how much it had cost him to maintain his dignity, contain his bitter anger. One by one people he had thought were friends had drifted from his life, uncomfortable with his pain, his altered circumstances, his initial lack of acceptance. So he understood Heather's reserve, her reluctance to trust again. He understood it because he shared it.

Disturbed by his thoughts, he consulted his watch again, his own anxiety increasing as the minutes ticked by.

'I think I'll telephone my parents in case there has been some mix up,' Heather announced, crossing to the side table.

He noticed how her hand shook as she lifted the receiver and dialled the number. Anxious eyes looked at him as the ringing tone went on, the call unanswered, and she finally set down the phone. They stared at each other for a moment, both jumping when the telephone rang, shrill and intrusive.

Simon was thinking again about all Heather had told him that afternoon, about his own feelings, and he missed her initial greeting to the caller. Then her sudden heart-rending cry speared into him.

'No! Please, no!'

As she swayed on her feet, Simon hurried to her, catching her just as the receiver fell from her nerveless fingers and she crumpled to the floor.

'Heather? Heather, can you hear me?'

Her eyes opened and focused on the man bending over her. Tears pricked her eyes.

'Amy,' she whispered, struggling to sit up.

'Stay where you are,' Simon instructed. 'You fainted. Give yourself a minute. Do you have some brandy? Anything?'

Wordlessly, Heather pointed towards the drinks cabinet across the room.

When Simon rose, she eased into an upright position.

'Here, sip this,' Simon advised, holding the glass for her.

Her gaze met his, drawing on his strength. She sipped the amber liquid, her eyes closing as it burned a fiery path down her throat.

'Do you feel up to talking?' he asked, his voice soft with concern.

Heather nodded, wanting to deny the horrific truth of what had happened.

'Simon, it's happening again. He has Amy.'

'What are you talking about?' he demanded in confusion. 'What's happened to Amy? Who has her?'

'James,' she managed, her voice edged with fear. 'It was James. He's taken Amy!'

Her stomach churned as she remembered the phone call, heard again the mocking delight in her former husband's vengeful words.

'I told you I would be back,' he had snarled. 'I told you that you were unfit to raise my daughter. Now she is mine. You'll never see her again, Heather. You can live the rest of your life wondering where she is. Now I have my revenge for your disloyalty.'

'How, Simon?' she cried. 'How did he get out? How did he find us?'

'Heather, slow down. You're not making sense.'

Her heart thudded in her chest, her breath coming in shallow gasps as fear for her precious daughter increased.

'I was a fool to believe I would ever be safe from him. Now he has Amy, again.'

Tears sliding down her cheeks, she struggled to her feet, swaying as her legs wobbled beneath her.

'Easy, sweetheart,' Simon murmured, beside her in an instant, supporting her.

'Murphy. Simon, I have to phone Murphy.'

'I'll help you,' he promised, crossing to the phone and carrying it back to her, flicking the long cord around the side of the sofa.

He held the phone for her while she tapped out the number. As she waited for the call to be answered, her nervous fingers knotted in the cord.

'Yes?'

She had never been so glad to hear that barked, Irish demand.

'Murphy. It's Amy. James has taken her. Murphy, please help me!

As Heather was clearly unable to continue, Simon took the phone.

'I'm a friend of Heather's,' he told the unknown man on the other end.

'What on earth is going on down there?'

For a moment Simon was taken aback by the gravelled, Irish voice, then he pulled himself together and filled him in as best he could. Heather had not been fully coherent with her explanations. He looked at her now, her tear-stained face pale and frightened, her whole body shaking.

'I'll be there within the hour,' the Irishman said when Simon had finished.

He was confused about the man's identity and place in Heather's life. Most of all he was concerned that the authorities be notified so they could begin the search for Amy straight away.

'What about the police?' Simon asked Murphy.

'I am the police, Mr Clarke.'

The call was abruptly disconnected. Simon stared at the receiver, a myriad questions buzzing in his mind, not the least of which was how had Murphy the policeman known his name?

By the time Murphy and the police arrived, Heather was sitting in an armchair cradling a cup of sweet tea in her hands. Simon had been wonderful. She didn't know how she would have survived the last hour or so without him. He had encouraged her to freshen up, providing unflagging support and encouragement. It had helped, more than she had thought possible, to share this trauma with someone else, some-one who, although he hadn't known her very long, cared so much about Amy.

Simon must have questions, Heather realised, but he kept them to himself, and she was grateful. She could not have stood any more. As it was, the terror and anxiety came over her in waves. A series of telephone calls had brought no response from her parents' house. Where were they? How had Amy been taken from them? Were they all safe?

The only time Simon had left her alone was to answer the entry phone, and now Murphy was here — Murphy O'Sullivan who had seen her and Amy through dark days once before. Could he do it again? Renewed tears welled in her eyes at the sight of him following Simon into the living-room. She rose unsteadily, hurried to greet the burly, grey-haired Irishman who had come to mean so much to Amy and herself.

'Murphy,' she cried.

'Come now, me dear.'

His voice was brusque, reflecting both his affection for her and his discomfort with displays of emotion.

'Sit down. We'll have the wee scoundrel back before you know it. Have I ever broken a promise to you now?'

'No, never. But, Murphy, what if — '

'No what-ifs, Heather. Let me do my job. I need the details.'

Heather gazed at Simon. He smiled his encouragement, his silent support. Drawing strength from him, in a halting voice she told Murphy, and the sergeant he called to join them, the events of the afternoon. When she had finished, Murphy patted her hand and rose to her feet.

'We'll put a tap on your phone, in case he calls again. The local force is checking on your parents, and we should have news soon.'

'I just don't understand, Murphy. What happened? How did James get here? How did he find us?'

'I'm waiting for answers to those questions myself,' he growled. 'You'll know when I do.'

Heather watched as the crusty

policeman cast a brooding, speculative look towards Simon, his steel grey graze curious and assessing.

'And will you be staying, Mr Clarke? Can I leave you to watch out for Heather?'

'Of course.'

Simon's quiet conviction, the determination in his voice as he met the older man's unspoken challenge, both warmed and worried Heather. Murphy nodded, apparently satisfied.

'I'll be away to the incident room. A constable will be staying here in the house, and there'll be a patrol outside. We'll find her, me dear.'

Simon could not help but wonder at the relationship between Heather and Murphy O'Sullivan. He wondered how she had a policeman on call, a high-ranking one, too, from what he had observed. With a feeling of deep unease, he guessed this had something to do with the past — the part of the past Heather had hinted at before the fateful call had come.

Heather seemed deflated when Murphy O'Sullivan had left. A feeling of helplessness settled over Simon. He wanted to help her. He wanted to hold her. They kept in constant touch with the police station through the policeman who remained at the house, but there was no news.

The birthday tea and Amy's pile of presents lay untouched in the kitchen. Simon saw them when he went to make fresh tea. A lump filled his throat as he thought of the nightmare Amy was going through, a nightmare they all shared in their own ways. After taking a mug of tea and a sandwich to the constable who had set up his post in the dining-room, Simon returned to Heather. Setting down two mugs of tea and a plate of food on the table beside the sofa, he looked down at her.

He had never seen anyone look so remote, so alone. He couldn't bear it, couldn't leave her like that, lost and afraid. He kneeled down beside her, hesitating a moment before he reached out and took her hand in his.

'Heather, you need to eat something.'

She shook her head.

'At least try to get some rest,' he cajoled. 'Nothing will happen without you knowing it, I promise you. But you need to maintain your reserves, sweetheart, for when Amy and your parents come home.'

'They will come home, won't they, Simon?'

'Yes. Yes, they'll come home.'

'I can't go through this again.'

Heather's whispered words brought a frown to his face. She had said something similar before in her shock after receiving the telephone call.

'Again?' he queried.

She nodded, her icy fingers clenching on his.

'James took Amy before.'

What kind of man would do this to a little girl? Simon fumed with rage.

'It's my fault. He's done this to punish me,' she added.

'Heather, no,' he protested. 'Don't do

this to yourself.'

'You don't understand.'

'Do you want to talk about it?' he asked gently.

Heather gave herself no time to wonder why she felt a sudden urge to talk to Simon. Perhaps by confiding in him about the past, when Amy had come safely home, she would be better able to handle the present. Aware of the warmth of his hand holding hers, drawing strength from his touch, and comfort from his presence, Heather met his steady gaze.

'I told you about James, the way our marriage was,' she began. 'When Amy was two, James was investigated by the police.'

'Why?' Simon asked in surprise.

'They suspected him of using his movements as a photographer to bring uncut diamonds into the country, part of a ring involving people in South Africa and Holland. He denied it, of course, but he had been under surveillance for some time. The police arrived early one morning with a warrant to search the house and his studio.'

'Did they find anything?'

'Yes. During a painstaking search, they turned the house upside down and discovered false rolls of film mixed with genuine ones. Inside the false rolls were cloth pouches containing raw crystals, a delivery James had yet to dispose of after his return from a shoot abroad the previous night. It was a huge shock. I had never suspected anything.

'I was standing in the hallway of our house, Amy in my arms, when all of a sudden, James broke away from the police upstairs. He thundered down, grabbed a knife from the kitchen, and tried to leave by the back door. But a policeman appeared there. James was desperate. And then he looked at me. I shrank back, afraid of what he would do. When he tried to take Amy from me, I resisted, and cried out to the police who were already coming down the stairs.'

Heather felt the press of tears, but

fought them away.

'James held the knife to my throat and threatened to hurt me if they came closer. I was so scared. At that moment, I believed he was capable of anything. Amy was screaming, and James kept trying to pull her from me. When I wouldn't let go, he hit out in a wild panic, cutting me, and I fell back against the stairs. Before I knew what had happened, he had taken Amy. I just lay there, dazed, beside myself as I heard her cries for me fading as James ran out of the house and down the path. And I couldn't do anything.'

She wiped her free hand across her eyes.

'James had Amy for six days before the police found them. For a while I wondered if I would ever see her again, and then, when I thought I would go mad with the waiting, it was over. Amy was back. He hadn't hurt her, not physically, but she was so subdued and withdrawn. I was over-protective from then on. I had mental scars, too, and perhaps we closed in on each other in a way that wasn't healthy. In the last weeks, Amy has begun to blossom again. I was so hopeful, really hopeful, for the first time in years. And now it's happening again.'

'You have nothing to reproach yourself for. Heather, listen to me,' Simon stressed, and she looked at him, at the steely determination in his gaze. 'The police found Amy once. They'll find her again.'

7

'You've been so good to me . . . to both of us, Simon,' Heather told him, buoyed by his reassurance. 'I don't know how to thank you.'

'You don't have to.'

His warm smile made her heart beat faster. Feeling overwhelmed, a little uncomfortable, she eased her hand from his and sat back, relieved when he accepted her withdrawal and the small distance she placed between them.

'So much happened after James was arrested,' she continued after a few moments. 'It didn't help that I testified against him, nor that I was subsequently granted sole custody of Amy. He made threats in court, blamed me for his downfall. Amy and I were given protection. We moved more times than I care to remember.'

Heather sighed, remembering that

difficult and unsettling time.

'And James went to prison?'

'Yes, for a long time, or so I thought. I can't believe he got out, or that he found us. I thought we had begun a new life. Now, because he wants revenge, he's taken my little girl again. Oh, Simon, is this ever going to be over? Am I ever going to be able to give Amy a normal life?'

Simon ached for her. The urge to take her in his arms was almost irresistible, but although the distance she had placed between them was small, it was a barrier, one she clearly was not ready for him to cross. It made his task all the harder. But learning of her past helped him understand the woman she was now. She had been hurt inside, was afraid to trust again, had suffered much at the hands of her former husband. Yet she had built a loving home for Amy, ran a successful business, was prepared to overcome her own fears for the sake of her daughter.

What worried him most now was

how both she and Amy would come through this a second time. But whatever happened, he determined he would be there to support and help them.

'You must rest,' he said now, his voice unusually husky. 'Can I help you upstairs, or would you rather stay down here?'

'Down here,' Heather murmured. 'I'll try to sleep.'

As she settled on the sofa, he left the room. After checking with the constable and learning there was no news, he went upstairs to locate the airing cupboard. He rummaged inside and found a warm blanket, then carried it back to the living-room. Heather's eyes were closed. He moved quietly, hoping she was asleep. But as he approached the sofa, the long lashed lids fluttered open.

'Is there any news?'

'No. I'm sorry.'

'I'm sorry to have gone to pieces like this,' she said softly.

'I think you're entitled.'

'I hate to be so useless.'

'You're a remarkable woman, Heather. A strong woman.'

'I'm not. I want to be doing something, anything. I just want my little girl.'

'I know, I know,' he said gently, hearing a fresh rise of panic in her voice. 'Murphy will find her.'

Switching off all but a couple of table lamps, Simon tucked the blanket around her, surprised when she reached out a hand, her fingers curling round his wrist.

'Thank you,' she whispered.

Simon felt a jolt from her touch, but he controlled his emotions.

'Would you mind staying with me?' she asked.

'I hadn't intended going anywhere,' he assured her with a smile.

When her fingers maintained their firm hold on him, he eased down on the floor, resting his back against the sofa. Her grip relaxed, and for some while

140

Simon stayed still and quiet, eyes closed, listening to the sound of her breathing. Absently, his free hand lifted and he massaged his shoulder.

'Are you uncomfortable?' The sound of her voice surprised him.

'It's nothing,' he excused, ignoring his aching joint.

'Are you sure?'

'Don't worry about it. Try and rest.'

She was silent for a few moments, then her voice came again, softer and more uncertain than ever.

'Simon?'

'Mm?'

'I — Could you — Will you please hold me?'

'Oh, Heather,' he whispered, a catch in his voice at her hesitant request. Ignoring the protest from his shoulder, he turned and moved beside her, careful to remember, even as he slid her into his arms, how difficult it must have been for her to ask for even this small physical contact.

Taking his time, keeping his hold

light and gentle, he soothed the fingers of one hand along her back, hoping to calm her, hoping she would realise his embrace was unthreatening. Keeping his own emotions under control, he couldn't help but savour this first opportunity to hold her. He breathed in the flowery scent of her, felt the silken texture of her hair against his skin. Slowly, he felt her acceptance. First it came in the gradual relaxing of her muscles, then in the way she turned ever so slightly towards him, seeking the comfort, the warmth, of another human being.

'Everything is going to be OK,' he murmured. 'I'm here for you.'

He felt the tremble in her body. Her breathing changed then caught as she struggled to control it, and then he felt the tears against his skin.

'Cry it out,' he encouraged.

As her tears flowed, his hand brushed the stray tendrils of hair and the salty wetness from her cheeks.

'Let it go, sweetheart.'

He held her until her sobs began to subside, giving her what strength and comfort he could. She burrowed close to him, exhausted, sleep claiming her at last. He couldn't say how long he lay there in the dimness, silent, alert, cradling her against him, wanting more than anything to take this nightmare from her. It was the constable who disturbed them in the early hours of the morning. A light knock at the door preceded his entry into the room.

Heather was awake instantly, jerking from his hold in alarm, as if she did not remember asking for it. Simon bit back his disappointment at her withdrawal, moving away from her to give her the space she needed. He watched as she swung her legs to the floor, her hands brushing her tousled hair from her tear-stained face.

'What is it?' she demanded, eagerness and fear mingled in her voice. 'Have they found Amy?'

'No, not yet. I'm sorry, Ms Marshall.' The constable paused. 'I've just had word that they have found your parents' car.'

'Murphy, what news is there?' Heather asked, on the telephone to the gruff Irishman within moments of the constable informing her that her parents' car had been found.

'Your parents are safe, Heather. They're safe now.'

'And Amy?' she whispered, hardly daring to hear the reply.

'Not yet. I'm sorry.'

Her initial euphoria abating, Heather glanced at Simon who waited nearby and shook her head. As thrilled as she was to learn the news of her parents, her anxiety increased for her precious daughter.

'What happened, Murphy? Are Mum and Dad all right?'

'They were shut in the boot of their car,' Murphy informed her, making her gasp in shock. 'Apart from being cramped and frightened, they were unharmed. They're being checked over at the hospital now, and I'll have them brought to your house as soon as possible.'

'Thank you.'

With trembling fingers, Heather replaced the receiver. Her voice husky with emotion, she related the details to Simon. Unable to meet his gaze, she rose to her feet. She paced the room, putting distance between them. She didn't want to think how it had felt to be held in Simon's arms, especially with Amy out there somewhere, frightened. It was so long since she had allowed herself any physical contact. She had asked for it, needed it, but it had still come as a shock. Being close to Simon, wrapped in his warmth, had been both comforting and disturbing.

Now, most of all, was not a time to become aware of his masculine appeal. Such a short while ago she had been convinced she was finished with all that, but the shock of Amy's disappearance had drawn her closer to Simon than she had ever intended to be.

'You don't have to stay, Simon,' she ventured now, a defensive note in her voice.

'I'm not leaving you.'

'I won't be alone. The policeman is here, and my parents will be coming. I've wallowed in self-pity long enough, Simon. I'm a big girl now, and more than able to take care of myself.'

'I know that.'

'Good. It will be dawn soon. I'm sure you want to get back to the school.

'No, Heather, that isn't what I want. Why are you pushing me away again? Can't you accept my friendship?'

'It's not that. I just can't think of anything but Amy.'

'I wasn't asking you to.'

He sounded so reasonable, so calm, and yet no matter what he said, something subtle had changed between them in the last few hours. She wasn't ready for it. She didn't know if she ever would be. Wrapping her arms around herself, she left the room.

Simon watched her go, feeling

frustrated at her withdrawal, the distance she was trying to put between them again. And yet he understood, ached for the uncertainty and lingering fear he saw in her eyes.

Upstairs, Heather removed her crumpled clothes and stood under the hot, stinging barbs of the shower. If only washing away this nightmare was as simple as removing the stiffness from her body. Towelling herself, she sat at her dressing-table and dried her hair, concentrating on the familiar task so that she wouldn't think of Amy and what she was going through, or what had happened to her parents. Also, she didn't want to think about Simon.

He had been so good to her, a tower of strength when she had needed it, comforting and understanding, but she didn't dare allow herself to rely on him, to come to care for him in any way. It cost too much. And it was a price she wasn't prepared to pay, ever again.

Dressed once more, she went downstairs and sought the sanctuary of her study, needing the space and the peace. For a while she stared unseeing at a shop file that lay opened on her desk, her mind drifting.

'Are you all right?'

Startled, she looked up and saw Simon framed in the doorway, a steaming mug cradled in his hands.

'Yes.'

Dragging her gaze from his, she closed the file and put it back in the drawer, nibbling at her lip when she spotted the dossier on Simon that Murphy had prepared for her.

'Can I get you a coffee?'

'No. Thank you. I don't want anything.'

Hesitating, her fingers closed on the envelope.

'Simon, I need to tell you something.'

He paused for a moment, then crossed to sit opposite her. Tense and nervous, she handed him the envelope, wondering at her own motives as she watched him look inside and saw the flare of anger cross his face.

'What is this?' he demanded.

Heather forced herself to meet his stormy gaze.

'In the beginning, when you took Amy to the hospital, I didn't know who you were. I asked Murphy to find out about you,' she admitted.

'I don't appreciate having my privacy invaded.'

He looked down at the copied pages for a moment, then slid them back in the envelope and passed it over to her.

'But,' he continued, his lids lifting to subject her to an intense, watchful stare, 'I can understand now why you were so cautious, so protective. And it also explains why Murphy knew my name when we met.'

Surprised by his acceptance, knowing how deeply he must have resented the knowledge of her intrusion into his private life, Heather felt at a loss.

'Why did you show me? I need never have known you had this,' he pointed out, a hint of understanding and thoughtfulness in his eyes.

'I've always felt uncomfortable about it. I thought you had a right to know.'

'Did you? Or was it a test, Heather? Were you hoping I would storm out of here and make it easy for you?'

It was only when he voiced the words that she recognised there was an element of truth in what he said. Lacking the strength to send him away, she had hoped to use his own anger at her to do it for her.

8

With the coming of dawn, Heather retreated outside to attend to Amy's guinea pigs. After giving them food and fresh water, she paused for a while in their run, cuddling their furry bodies to her. It made her feel closer to her daughter. A renewed welling of tears stung her eyes.

She sensed rather than heard Simon's approach. Setting the guinea pigs back on the grass, she wiped her eyes, gathering some composure before she turned round.

'Your parents are here. They're waiting for you in the living-room,' he told her when she joined him on the lawn. 'You go on in. I'll shut up here.'

'Thank you.'

Heather ran into the house, her feet echoing a tattoo along the hallway as she sped along to the living-room.

Looking tired, drawn and shaky, her parents rushed to greet her. After several moments during which they enjoyed a tearful hug, Heather ushered them to the sofa.

'Are you sure you are both unhurt?' she asked.

'Quite sure,' her father replied. 'What about you? How are you coping?'

'I'll be all right,' Heather attempted with a smile.

Before she could ask any more, Simon arrived with a tray of coffee which he set on the table by the sofa.

'Thank you, Simon.'

Heather felt a warmth in her face as she met the curiosity in her parents' eyes. She took a deep breath, and made the introductions.

'Simon, we're so pleased to meet you, and can't thank you enough for all you have done,' her mother said. 'Amy told us so much about you.'

A silence settled at the mention of the little girl's name, and tears sprung to Elizabeth Marshall's eyes.

'Heather, we're so sorry about what's happened. We feel responsible.'

'Oh, Mum, don't,' Heather interrupted, aghast. 'It wasn't your fault, neither of you. Don't ever think that.'

'James just appeared out of nowhere,' her father explained, 'when we arrived back at the house, and snatched Amy before we realised what was happening. He forced us to get into the boot of the car, then drove off. When the car stopped, we heard the doors bang shut, then the sound of another car engine fading in the distance. That was the last we knew until the police found us.'

Listening to her father, Heather shuddered at their horrifying experience.

'I'm just so relieved to have you here,' she murmured, hugging them.

Simon watched them all together. As much as he hated to leave Heather, with her parents there, he had no reason to stay.

'I'd best be going,' he announced,

hiding his reluctance with difficulty. 'I need a shower, a shave and a change of clothes.'

Heather walked with him to the door, unwilling to examine the welter of emotions that coursed through her. She had wanted him to leave, but now the time had come, she was sorry to lose the comfort he had given, and the link he provided to Amy. But it was more than that, and it was that part that troubled her.

'I'm grateful, Simon.'

He stilled further words, resting a finger tip against her lips.

'Don't,' he instructed softly.

His dark eyes regarded her, something that could have been yearning flickering in their depths before he masked it. Disturbed by his touch, Heather raised a hand, her fingers closing round the span of his wrist, confusion reflected in her eyes.

'I'll be in touch,' he promised. 'You'll call me if there's any news or if you need anything, even just to talk.'

'Yes,' Heather confirmed, her voice husky.

He hesitated a moment more, then before she could react, he bent to brush a warm kiss across her cheek. Then he was gone. Heather leaned against the closed door, her fingers pressed to the spot he had kissed, her skin still tingling from his touch.

Before she rejoined her parents, Heather acknowledged a brief moment of fear. Yes, most of all there was fear for her daughter's safety, but a new fear was beginning to percolate through her. A fear that Simon was becoming ever more important to both her present and her future. Heather had plenty of time to think about Simon over the next few hours — too much time, and she resented his intrusion when she really wanted to devote all her energies into finding Amy.

Her parents, recovering from their own ordeal, had stayed to support her, her father going home only to fetch a fresh change of clothes for himself and his wife. Heather was grateful for their presence. She didn't want to be alone, with only the police constable on duty for company.

More times than she cared to admit she had almost picked up the telephone to call Simon, just to hear his voice. Aside from herself and her parents, he was the next person closest to Amy, the only other person with whom she could share this trauma. And yet she hesitated seeking the comfort he could give, because she was afraid of becoming too dependent on him, too close to him.

Her manageress rang to update her on the boutique but Heather found it difficult to turn her mind to business matters, although it was the business that sustained her. Now, nothing mattered but Amy.

Heather closed her eyes, a shiver running through her. She felt so helpless, frustrated at leaving everything to the police and unable to do anything constructive. The threats James had made continued to haunt her. No matter how she tried to be positive and comforted by the reassurance of her parents, Simon and Murphy O'Sullivan, the lingering fear remained.

What if she never saw Amy again?

★   ★   ★

Simon sat in his car in a field gateway along from Heather's house, wondering for the umpteenth time what he was doing. She had promised to phone if there was news, or if she needed anything, but he hadn't been able to leave it at that.

It had been two days now since he had seen her, and aside from his anxiety for Amy and for Heather, the simple truth was that he missed her. He knew she was afraid, he even knew what she was afraid of — trust, intimacy, letting down the barriers. He understood, because he shared it.

Such a short time ago, he, too, had been determined he would never again let anyone close enough to hurt him, but almost without him knowing it, Amy, then her mother, had slipped past his guard and lodged themselves in his heart.

Turn round and go home, a voice inside his head instructed him. His fingers tightened on the steering wheel. He could no more walk away from her than he could stop breathing. He needed to be close to her, needed to feel he could do something to help her through this nightmare.

Losing his inner battle, he put the car in gear and drove the remaining distance to Heather's home. The police constable responded to the ring of the entry phone, and before he could change his mind, Simon drove through the gates, watching as they closed behind him.

'Simon's here.'

Startled by her father's softly-spoken words, Heather spun round, trying to ignore the unsteady rhythm of her heart.

'Your mother has gone to meet him at the door.'

He paused a moment, watching her.

'He seems a nice man.'

'Yes. He's been good to Amy. She's fond of him.'

'And you?'

'What about me?'

From the corner of her eye, she saw him smile.

'I know you so well, Heather, how you think, what you feel, and I love you. I want you to be happy. Don't let what James has done, now and in the past, ruin the rest of your life. If you do, he's won. When Amy is back with us, think about your future, and about yourself. You'd be a fool if you let that man slip away.'

It was one of the longest speeches she had heard her father make, and one that gave her much pause for thought. She met his gaze, seeing his love for her, his concern, the strength of his conviction. Her reply was forestalled by the arrival of her mother, Simon behind her, already carrying a tea tray! He set down the tray and greeted her father.

When he turned to Heather, his eyes warm and intense, she felt a tingle down her spine. Turning away, annoyed and confused by her reaction, she thrust thoughts of him aside, unable to be diverted in any way from Amy.

Heather looked strained and pale, but still hauntingly beautiful, Simon thought. She had barely acknowledged him, but at least she had not told him to leave. Watching her from beneath his lashes, he thought back to his arrival, to his talk with her mother in the kitchen while they made the tea.

'Has Heather told you about James?' Elizabeth Marshall had asked him.

'Yes, she spoke of him, of her marriage.'

'It's not something she normally confides,' Elizabeth said in surprise.

'I know that, but I'm glad that she did. It helped me to understand so many things.'

'You care about her, don't you, Simon?'

'Of course,' he had replied warily. 'It's a terrible time.'

'I didn't mean that, young man. You care about my daughter very much, more than you'll admit to me, and maybe more than you know yourself. I think you need each other.'

The final remark had made him uncomfortable, and now it continued to make him think, about himself, about Heather, about dreams that had been shattered and consigned to the past. Elizabeth Marshall saw too much. He wondered how much Heather had told her parents about him, and thought again of the file she had in her desk, the file that detailed his painful past. He understood why she had obtained the information, but he still didn't like it.

'Tell us about yourself, Simon,' Tony Marshall invited now, cutting across his thoughts.

'Dad, I'm sure Simon could do without the third degree,' Heather intervened, the lightness she ~~placed~~ in her voice failing to hide the

Simon looked at her, askin~~g~~ ~~a silent~~ question. She shook her head, confirming she had told them nothing of the contents of the file.

Tony Marshall looked from one to the other.

'I didn't mean to pry. I was interested, I admit, and I thought it would help us all to talk of something else.'

'It's all right, I don't mind,' Simon surprised himself by saying. 'What did you want to know?'

'Have you always been a teacher?' Elizabeth Marshall asked.

'No. No, I was involved in sport for some time.'

He paused, his gaze going to Heather who sat opposite, watching him.

'I had an accident, and it was after that that I turned to teaching.'

He waited for the usual reaction, the dawning of recognition, the moment when the penny dropped, followed by the questions. But it never came. Instead, Heather's parents smiled encouragingly at him, warm and friendly, accepting. Unconsciously, he rubbed at his sore shoulder, memories swirling around him. He saw the understanding in Heather's eyes, remembered her courage, and before he realised what he was doing, he was giving them an edited version of his story.

Heather listened to Simon recount the bare facts of what she knew of his life. It was typically modest, playing down his genuine heroism, the extent of his pain, all that he had lost, but she knew, and she ached for him. As she watched him, she wondered if he was aware how often he rubbed his shoulder, wondered more how much pain he still endured.

She realised, for the first time, how alike they were in some ways, and he had intuitively been drawn to Amy and to herself. She felt sorry for him when he finished talking. He looked drained, stunned almost at what he had revealed about himself. That, too, she understood, remembering how she had confided in him about her past, how she had felt talking about things for the first time.

'Simon, could you help me with the guinea pigs?' Heather asked, rising to her feet, determined to give him some breathing space before her well-meaning but persistent parents could ask any more questions.

He sent her a relieved smile.

'I'd be glad to.'

As he rose to his feet and accompanied her from the room, Heather was conscious of his presence beside her.

'Thank you,' he murmured as they walked through the kitchen.

'What for?'

'You know.'

Heather opened the gate of the guinea pigs' run and stepped inside.

'You didn't have to tell them anything.'

'I know.'

He caught Ginger and Patch, and handed the furry bundles to her.

'Somehow it felt right. Here, you hold them, I'll clean out the hutch.'

Heather hugged the pets to her and watched in silence as Simon worked, wondering if he had found the experience of speaking of his past as daunting yet soothing as she had done. With fresh shavings, hay, food and water ready for them, Heather put her charges in the hutch for the night and shut the door. Turning, she saw Simon set the bucket down outside, his hand lifting to his shoulder.

'It still troubles you, doesn't it?'

'Sometimes,' he admitted, withdrawing his hand, his gaze avoiding hers. 'Nothing to worry about.'

He knew he was making light of his real discomfort, but she didn't press the subject. Instead, with her fingers hooked on the wire mesh of the run, she looked at the guinea pigs chattering happily in their hutch, her thoughts on Amy.

'She'll come home, Heather,' he told her, his voice soft but strong. 'Everything will be all right.'

'I want to believe that, Simon. I have to believe it. It's just so hard.'

She sensed him hesitate for a moment, then he reached out and covered one of her hands with his.

'I can't begin to imagine what you must be going through because I'm not a parent, but I care about Amy. I care about all of you. If you need anything, I'm here.'

Touched by his words, she managed to smile her thanks, holding back a sudden threat of tears.

Simon bit back the things he wanted to say, like how beautiful she was, how much stronger and more resilient than she realised, how much she had achieved for Amy and herself, how incredible her eyes were, how much he yearned to hear her laugh, how he yearned to hold her, to kiss her. But he couldn't say any of it yet. He could only hope that one day soon, he would.

A shout from the house roused them both from their separate reveries.

'Heather! Simon!'

Tony and Elizabeth Marshall appeared at the back door, waving excitedly and talking at once.

'Come quickly. Murphy is on the phone. He's found out where James has taken Amy!'

It seemed only minutes later that Heather was settled in the bucket seat of Simon's sports car and they were on their way to Oxfordshire. With her parents' car impounded for police forensic checks, it had been the obvious thing for Tony and Elizabeth Marshall to wait behind and for her to go with Simon. She could have waited for a police car, but she could not bear another second of delay.

Impatience and anxiety gripped her, and fear mingled with hope that she would soon be reunited with her daughter. The details from Murphy had been sketchy, just enough to make her believe the end was in sight and to have her rushing from the house, no other thought in her mind.

Her fingers knotted in her lap. She felt coiled like a spring, ready to burst at any moment, her throat constricted, her chest tight, her heartbeat rapid and heavy beneath her ribs. The atmosphere inside the car seemed to crackle, the silence stretching, each lost in anxious anticipation.

'How long will it take to get there?' she asked, her voice sounding hoarse and strained.

'Half an hour, no more. It depends on the traffic.'

Heather lapsed into silence.

'What else did he say on the phone?' Simon asked after a while.

Heather frowned, pressing the fingers of one hand to her temple where a tension headache was forming.

'Just that they've found an address where they think James is holding Amy. They are waiting for me to get there before they move.'

Please, she offered in silent prayer.

Please don't let it be a false alarm. Please let my little girl be safe.

Simon drove as fast as was safe, cursing the traffic, the darkness, the wet and murky conditions. He was thankful he had been there when the call had come. Heather seemed oblivious to his presence now, but he hoped his being there would help her in some way. He glanced across at her, her profile shadowed in the dim interior of the car. Even in this light she looked pale and drawn, the stress of the last few days taking their toll on her.

By the time they arrived at the small, country police station where Murphy was waiting for them, Heather was sure her frayed nerves would snap. Light spilled from every window, and the small carpark at the side was bursting with police vehicles. She was shaking when she left the car, grateful for the support that Simon offered on the walk to the entrance. Inside, the station was crowded, but when she gave her name, a path appeared between the waiting policemen and women, and she walked with Simon towards an office at the back.

'You're here. Good,' Murphy greeted them with characteristic gruffness, waving them to chairs.

He closed the door and walked round the desk, where he opened a file.

'Here's what we have now.'

He drew a chair up to the desk and sat down, heavy brows drawn together as he concentrated on the notes in front of him. Heather waited with increasing impatience, her nails digging into the palms of her hands. Murphy looked up, lips pursed.

'We checked the prison records, and came up with two leads. James had two visitors who interested us. One, a man by the name of David Worthington, is a dubious private investigator. He needs money, and doesn't ask questions. He was hired to find you.'

'And the other visitor?' Heather asked when Murphy paused.

'A woman, Victoria Baines. She's a

prison visitor and fell for his sob story and the charm. We believe she helped James take Amy, and we believe they are holed up at the old mill cottage a few miles from here.'

When Simon reached out a hand to her, Heather took it, seeing his warmth and his strength as his fingers curled with hers.

'How did Marshall get out of prison?' Simon wanted to know.

'He absconded on a hospital visit. He made his way to the woman's cottage, paid off Worthington for the information, and planned his move. He was clever, but not clever enough.'

Murphy closed the file with a snap and rose to his feet.

'Now, me dear, are you ready to go and get that wee scoundrel of yours?'

Heather blinked back the tears, relief and anger and nervous tension threatening to overcome her.

'Yes, I'm ready, Murphy. More than ready.'

'What's taking them so long?'

Heather's plaintive whisper sounded loud in the silent darkness. Simon slipped his arm around her, shielding her from the drizzle and the cold as they huddled by the police cars at the bottom of the lane that led to Victoria Baines' cottage.

'They know what they're doing,' he murmured back, his reassurance sounding more confident than he felt. 'It won't be much longer now.'

He understood her impatience. They had been waiting here for what seemed an eternity, two police officers nearby, the rest setting the trap and encircling the cottage. Through the trees, Simon could see a light in a downstairs window, a faint curl of smoke rising from a chimney and curling up to mingle with the curtain of mist.

Was Amy there? Was she safe? He prayed everything would go to plan and she and Heather would be together soon. Anything else could not be contemplated. Hiding his thoughts, wanting only to comfort and protect the woman who had infiltrated his heart, he drew her more closely against him.

'It'll be all right, Heather.'

Simon's closeness and his confident words gave her strength. It was so tempting to just run to the cottage, force her way in, search for her daughter, but she knew she couldn't. Simon was right. She had to let the police do their job.

A police radio crackled nearby, making her jump, her body tensing, ready to move. Both she and Simon instinctively moved closer to the two policemen who stood nearby, but nothing was said, no news was given.

How long could this go on? She wrung her hands together, numb with cold, not sure she could have gone on waiting had Simon not supported her, both physically and mentally. She was frightened how much he had come to mean to her over the last days.

'Heather.'

Something in the way he said her name alerted her. There was no other noise, no warning. She looked up, followed the direction of his gaze, and made out a shape coming towards them in the gloom. The figure was indistinct, the movement purposeful as it closed the gap between them.

It was a man, Heather realised — Murphy. And he carried something in his arms.

'Amy?'

Heather broke from Simon's hold and began to run, sobs of relief robbing her of breath.

'Amy!'

'Mummy! Mummy!'

Oblivious of the wet mud, Heather sank to her knees on the track, opening her arms as Murphy set Amy on her feet. Tears streaming down her cheeks, Heather enfolded her daughter in her arms.

9

'How soon will it be until they come?' Amy kept asking impatiently and Heather smiled and drew the little girl on to her lap for a hug.

'Another couple of hours. The time will soon pass,' she said gently in response to her daughter's plaintive sigh.

Amy wriggled to free herself, and Heather let her go, watching as she paced across the study. It was a joy just to watch her, to know that she was home, safe, well.

For the first few days after they had been reunited that cold, wet night in Oxfordshire, Heather had kept a careful watch on her daughter, anxiously looking for any warning signs, any evidence of reaction following her ordeal. But to Heather's relief, Amy had coped remarkably well. She had been quiet at first, clinging, very tired, but after a week, she had begun to settle.

The process, begun before James had snatched her, continued, with Amy blossoming and emerging from her shell. Heather offered up countless prayers of thanks, loving the mischievous, bubbly character Amy was becoming, proud of her daughter for her resilience, her courage.

When she had suggested that Amy might like to have a Christmas party, she had not imagined the little girl would accept with such enthusiasm. Taken aback, delighted, she watched as Amy made her own invitations to half a dozen of her new playmates. Her special companion was Jilly Walker, the classmate whose tentative approach the day of the school outing had seen the start of an enduring friendship.

'Can I put on my dress yet?' Amy asked, skipping excitedly back to Heather's side.

'In a little while. You don't want to spoil it.'

Amy hung on her arm and leaned back, swinging from side to side.

'Why don't you go and see Patch and Ginger? You can tell them about your party,' Heather suggested, remembering the excited impatience of childhood.

'OK. Can I take some carrots?'

Heather smoothed down the strands of Amy's hair.

'All right, but no touching any of the party food when you're in the kitchen,' she added with a mock stern frown. 'Deal?'

'Mummy!' Amy giggled in delight. 'Deal, I promise.'

'Go on then, and put your coat on. It's cold out there.'

Heather looked out of the window across the frosted garden, and watched as Amy undid the door of the hutch and small run that had been prepared for the guinea pigs' winter quarters. Heather's thoughts returned to the events of the last few weeks.

Inevitably, her thoughts lingered on Simon. He had been a rock, an unbelievable support to her during that terrible time, and she had come to rely on him and care for him far more deeply than she had ever realised. So much so that his absence from her life for the last month had been dreadful. She would never have believed how much she would miss him, the sight of him, the sound of his voice, his care, his companionship.

Troubled, she turned from the windows and closed the shop accounts she had been working on. Why had he stayed away? Had he just been there for her because of Amy? She was so confused, her emotions all jumbled.

Amy had seen him at school. She still talked of him endlessly, but Heather hadn't even had so much as a glimpse of him in the distance. Was he avoiding her? Why? She had been tempted, oh, so tempted, to telephone him, but nervous uncertainty had held her back.

Simon was the most amazing man

she had ever met. He was sensitive to her needs, understanding, compassionate, warm. He, too, had lived through so much, overcome so much, and yet he still gave of himself. She had never wanted to care for him, had never expected to care for anyone again, not after James. She was afraid of opening herself up again, of being hurt.

Her thoughtful frown deepened. She missed him with the kind of hollow ache that gave her no rest. She knew now that Simon had become more important to her than her fear of the past.

The telephone rang, jolting her from her thoughts. She picked up the receiver.

'Hello?'

'And Happy Christmas to you, me dear.'

'Murphy!' A smile brightened her features. 'How are you? It's been a while.'

'Indeed, indeed. I'm fine. And yourself? The wee scoundrel?'

Heather's gaze strayed back to the garden.

'We're fine, Murphy. Amy's brilliant. I can't believe how well she's handled everything.'

'She takes after her mother.'

'I don't have her courage.'

Murphy replied with a sharp sound of derision.

'What nonsense you're talking.'

He paused for a moment.

'Are you all right with everything,' he asked at length.

'Yes.'

Heather knew he was referring to James. It had been Murphy who had telephoned her with the latest news two weeks ago, explaining how James had tried to escape again, breaking free of the guards who were taking him to court. Running across a main road, he had been hit by a bus.

She regretted the loss of life, the waste, the whole tragedy of the past. She had also felt guilty for the flicker of relief that the fear had been lifted from her present and her future. There would be no more fear for Amy, no more looking over their shoulders for danger, no more security fences.

Finally it was over. She and Amy had the rest of their lives to look forward to. What she now had to decide was what form that life should take. Did she want the safe option, being alone? Could she learn to love and trust again?

'Have a wonderful holiday, Heather,' Murphy said now, voice gruff to hide his affection. 'New year, new start. Make the most of it, you hear? May you be happy, you deserve it . . . all of you.'

After he had rung off, Heather wondered at the emphasis he had placed on the words, all of you. Did he know? Was he telling her something?

Amy bounded back indoors, excited, full of life, and Heather went upstairs with her to get ready for the party. She brushed the little girl's hair until it gleamed, framing the cherubic face like a shining halo. She looked beautiful in her new dress, red tartan with black velvet trimming, matching ribbons in her hair, and shiny black shoes on her feet.

Before they knew it, the house was filled with children's laughter and chatter. Each room had a warm glow, festooned with decorations, lights, warmth. For the first time, it felt to Heather like a real home. A huge Christmas tree, decked with multi-coloured tinsel, bright, shiny balls, and a string of lights, dominated one corner of the living-room. Heather watched, a smile of pure joy on her face, as the children played.

'Who's ready for some tea?' Heather asked, laughing as a chorus of voices erupted and eager faces turned towards her.

She led the way to the kitchen, noting how Amy glanced at the front door and the clock in the hall, a flash of disappointment on her face.

'What's up?' she whispered to her daughter.

'Nothing,' Amy murmured, smothering a sigh as she took her place at the table.

While Heather was pouring glasses of juice, the doorbell rang.

'I'll get it,' Amy yelled, slithering off her chair and dashing down the corridor before Heather could gather her wits.

Laughing with the children as she sorted out plates, Heather glanced up as Amy returned, a beaming smile of triumph on her face. Heather froze in shock. Behind her daughter was Simon!

'Father Christmas was busy, so I'm delivering these for him,' Simon announced as he walked into the kitchen carrying a sack of presents.

He'd registered Heather immediately, felt the kick in his stomach at the sight of her after four weeks of forcing himself to stay away. He focused on the children, giving himself time to compose his wayward emotions. Eager hands took the packages he handed round the table, and cries of delight mingled with the sounds of tearing wrapping paper. A toy sitting by each place, the children resumed their tea.

'What will you have, Simon?'

He allowed his gaze to rest on Heather. She was even more beautiful than before, an excitement about her, something else that was different that he couldn't define. Then he realised. The fear was gone from those eyes. Her worst nightmare was over, the shadow had been lifted from her.

'Tea would be good, thanks.' He smiled, responding to her question. 'May I help?'

'Just keep an eye on the table!'

Simon ached to talk to her, to hold her, but perhaps having the children there would give him and Heather time to adjust to seeing each other again. She was edgy, nervous, but not like she had been before. He couldn't define it, but she had been surprised to see him. And pleased? He wasn't sure.

Helping himself to a piece of cake, and taking the seat Amy had drawn up for him next to her, Simon joined in with the general chatter. But he watched Heather. He had wondered if he would ever hear her laugh.

Now she was smiling and joking, deriving as much enjoyment from the jokes and games as the children themselves. And she laughed. He couldn't describe what the sound did to him. He would never tire of hearing it, never tire of looking at her. When tea was over, he would talk to her. Four weeks was long enough. He had to know.

Heather was painfully conscious of Simon's presence, his laugh, his special way with the children. It had felt that her world had brightened when he had walked through the door, and her instant reaction could not be ignored. When tea came to an end, she sent the children through to the living-room to play some games, then, unaccountably nervous, she drew in a breath and faced him.

'Amy invited me,' he said, his gaze

lingering on her, warm and assessing. 'You didn't know?'

'No.'

'Are you sorry I came?'

Heather licked her lips.

'No,' she admitted, voice husky, wondering why it was suddenly so hard to breathe. 'We haven't seen you for a while.'

'I always intended coming back, Heather. I was giving you the thinking space I thought you needed.'

'I have been thinking.'

He moved closer to her, making her more aware of him.

'And?'

'I'm scared.'

'Of me?'

He frowned, his eyes darkening.

'No, of me, of everything, I suppose.'

She clenched her hands to halt their nervous shaking.

'Of taking another chance,' she added.

Simon nodded, folding his arms across his chest.

'I've been there, too. After Eileen, I

vowed I would never get involved again, never allow myself to be hurt any more. We're two of a kind, you and I. We could help each other.'

'You've given me and Amy so much, Simon.'

'No more than you've given me.'

'I've done nothing,' she protested, confused.

He took another step closer, reaching out to trail the fingers of one hand down her cheek.

'Yes, you have. You've given me a reason to hope. You've given me back my life. Let me share it with you.'

Heather found it hard to think with him so close, the touch of his fingers making her skin tingle and spreading fire through her veins.

'But — '

His finger on her lips silenced her.

'The past can't hurt us any more, Heather. We've both had dreams broken, but we can make new ones, together. I love you. I love Amy. I want us to be together, to give us all another chance at happiness.'

Heather gazed into the depths of his eyes, seeing his love, hearing his words. How could he reach inside to the vulnerable part of her? He touched her soul, and he made her whole. He had been right. They needed each other.

Through the house, the sound of children's laughter rang out and brought tears to her eyes, tears of joy, hope and love. Looking at Simon, she knew. If she had the courage to reach out and take it, happiness and the future could be hers. Her throat clogged on emotion, choking off words.

His hand moved again, sliding along the curve of her neck, his fingers sinking into the silken fall of her hair. A smile came unbidden when he reached to his pocket and held up a sprig of mistletoe.

'May I kiss you?'

A twinkle of mischief shone in his eyes, but deeper, and far more important, there lingered a serious intent. Heather recognised it, recognised his question.

This wasn't just about a kiss, it was about them, their lives, together, for ever. Her answer was clear and sure. Looking at him through tear-bright eyes, she smiled.

'Yes.'

For a second, he hesitated, then exultation replaced disbelief. His mouth met hers, tentative, questing, warm and firm. With a sigh at the rightness of it, Heather's lips parted for him, welcoming, deepening the kiss, sealing their pact. The wave of love, of need, she felt was almost too much. She, who had feared this, knew she would never be afraid again.

'Your mummy and Mr Clarke are kissing,' Jilly Walker exclaimed in awe.

'What? Let me see,' Amy hissed.

A door hinge creaked as she moved for a better view.

'Yes! I told you, Jilly,' she confided in satisfaction. 'This is going to be the best Christmas ever! We're going to be a family.'

We do hope that you have enjoyed reading this large print book.

Did you know that all of our titles are available for purchase?

We publish a wide range of high quality large print books including:
Romances, Mysteries, Classics
General Fiction
Non Fiction and Westerns

Special interest titles available in large print are:
The Little Oxford Dictionary
Music Book, Song Book
Hymn Book, Service Book

Also available from us courtesy of Oxford University Press:
Young Readers' Dictionary
(large print edition)
Young Readers' Thesaurus
(large print edition)

For further information or a free brochure, please contact us at:
Ulverscroft Large Print Books Ltd.,
The Green, Bradgate Road, Anstey,
Leicester, LE7 7FU, England.
Tel: (00 44) **0116 236 4325**
Fax: (00 44) **0116 234 0205**

CONVALESCENT HEART

Lynne Collins

They called Romily the Snow Queen, but once she had been all fire and passion, kindled into loving by a man's kiss and sure it would last a lifetime. She still believed it would, for her. It had lasted only a few months for the man who had stormed into her heart. After Greg, how could she trust any man again? So was it likely that surgeon Jake Conway could pierce the icy armour that the lovely ward sister had wrapped about her emotions?

TOO MANY LOVES

Juliet Gray

Justin Caldwell, a famous personality of stage and screen, was blessed with good looks and charm that few women could resist. Stacy was a newcomer to England and she was not impressed by the handsome stranger; she thought him arrogant, ill-mannered and detestable. By the time that Justin desired to begin again on a new footing it was much too late to redeem himself in her eyes, for there had been too many loves in his life.

MYSTERY AT MELBECK

Gillian Kaye

Meg Bowering goes to Melbeck House in the Yorkshire Dales to nurse the rich, elderly Mrs Peacock. She likes her patient and is immediately attracted to Mrs Peacock's nephew and heir, Geoffrey, who farms nearby. But Geoffrey is a gambling man and Meg could never have foreseen the dreadful chain of events which follow. Throughout her ordeal, she is helped by the local vicar, Andrew Sheratt, and she soon discovers where her heart really lies.

HEART UNDER SIEGE

Joy St Clair

Gemma had no interest in men — which was how she had acquired the job of companion/secretary to Mrs Prescott in Kentucky. The old lady had stipulated that she wanted someone who would not want to rush off and get married. But why was the infuriating Shade Lambert so sceptical about it? Gemma was determined to prove to him that she meant what she said about remaining single — but all she proved was that she was far from immune to his devastating attraction!